A c
was be
the art of stalking men. He slid the hinge-framed Smith & Wesson American out of leather and eared back the hammer.

Crrrick! No farther than a few feet away the ratcheting of the sear notches on a Cole hammer paralyzed the Kid for a second. Then reflexively, he fired in the direction of the sound.

"Damn, that hurts."

Reprieve swelled through the Kid's chest. With one opponent down he had a chance. He covered thirty yards safely when a bullet cracked past him.

"The next one goes in the back of your head," a husky voice informed him.

The Kid had no choice — he had to make a break. He made it within five feet of his horse when a terrible pain exploded in his right leg. All of a sudden his Smith became too heavy to hold. And something had happened to his vision. Was he really seeing a girl bending over him?

Charity Rose quickly recovered his six-gun and located her hat. Long auburn hair tucked safely out of sight, she went to aid Cliff Collins. He sat with his back against a boulder. With both hands he held shut the entry wound.

"I was lucky," the young policeman informed her. "It didn't hit the artery. You're a mighty fine partner, C.M. Ain't many men good as you, I guess."

Unaccountable, to Cliff Collins's way of things, the young bounty hunter blushed fleetingly. "That's a bigger compliment than you thought," she said sincerely.

WHITE SQUAW
Zebra's Adult Western Series
by E. J. Hunter

#1: SIOUX WILDFIRE	(1205, $2.50)
#3: VIRGIN TERRITORY	(1314, $2.50)
#4: HOT TEXAS TAIL	(1359, $2.50)
#5: BUCKSKIN BOMBSHELL	(1410, $2.50)
#12: BALL AND CHAIN	(1930, $2.50)
#13: TRACK TRAMP	(1995, $2.50)
#14: RED TOP TRAMP	(2075, $2.50)

Available wherever paperbacks are sold, or order direct from the Publisher. Send cover price plus 50¢ per copy for mailing and handling to Zebra Books, Dept. 2490, 475 Park Avenue South, New York, N.Y. 10016. Residents of New York, New Jersey and Pennsylvania must include sales tax. DO NOT SEND CASH.

E. J. HUNTER

#5 MILE-HIGH MADAM

**ZEBRA BOOKS
KENSINGTON PUBLISHING CORP.**

Special acknowledgements to Mark K. Roberts.

ZEBRA BOOKS

are published by

Kensington Publishing Corp.
475 Park Avenue South
New York, NY 10016

Copyright © 1988 by E. J. Hunter

All rights reserved. No part of this book may be reproduced in any form or by any means without the prior written consent of the Publisher, excepting brief quotes used in reviews.

First printing: October, 1988

Printed in the United States of America

This volume in the saga of Charity Rose is dedicated to Rowena Carter, who has become as big a fan as her husband, Bernie. As they say in Chinese restaurants, "Enjoy!"

EJH

Chapter 1

High in the cerulean sky of western Colorado, a giant black buzzard folded its white-barred wings and plummeted toward a pair of writhing black mounds in a gentle swale of the prairie. Another pair of eyes had discerned death. Glinting a slitted green, they observed the newcomer's arrival as it landed in a controlled crash. Recovering composure it waddled toward the squirming mass of black feathers.

The buzzard ignored a gallery of scolding crows and ducked a murderous slash from a competitor. Then it dove in to hack off a chunk of putrid flesh in its powerful beak. The blast of a high-powered rifle interrupted the grisly feast. Carrion birds scattered in every direction. The most heavily fed had to make long, clumsy runs to become airborne, flat feet slapping puffs of dust. The substance of the banquet appeared to be a man and a burro. Both were incongruously separated from their heads, both quivered from strange internal spasms.

Nimble fingers flipped a lever, dropped the breech of a Marlin Pacific rifle and extracted a smoking shell. Then they inserted a fresh .45-70 cartridge. Again the hollow bellow, this time followed by the slap of 450 grains of flat-nosed lead striking burro flesh. From their chest cavities, both cadavers explosively disgorged blood-smeared black horrors, which lumbered into awkward flight as a huge gray and silver wolf dog charged after them.

Again reloading the Marlin, a slender black-clad figure rose from the buffalo grass and emitted a shrill whistle. It was immediately echoed by the high-pitched whinny of a horse. A coal-black stallion, with matching silver-mounted saddle, cantered over the rise, head held sideways to avoid the dangling reins.

"Easy, Lucifer, steady big boy," came the strange, raspy voice of the animal's master as the Marlin slid into its rear-slung scabbard. Small, black-gloved hands unknotted a silk bandana from a surprisingly slender throat, then fetched a canteen from the horn and soaked the scarf.

"Stay here, boy. Yonder's no place for your sensitive nose." So saying, the rider hitched up a pair of ebon-handled Colt Bisley revolvers in an ornately carved buscadero rig and started afoot toward the carnage.

"Thig, Butch!" The wolf dog came bounding to

the gun hawk's side.

Together, the pair made their investigation. Like many who lived much of their lives in the wilderness, C. M. Rose spoke to animals like they were people. Not too surprisingly, these four-footed denizens of the prairie often listened and reacted as though they understood every word.

"Look here, boy," came the husky whisper. "The poor fellow was preparing a meal. Beans and moldy bacon; coffee container's empty, but he brewed tea from calomel weed."

Upon finding a short-handled pick and shovel, the black-clad rider stooped to recover them, then began to dig a shallow grave. Straining against the hard, dry ground, C. M. Rose contemplated the decapitated victims.

"Seems I recall a notice in the Trail City newspaper. Right beside the eulogy to Print Olive, I think. An axe murderer. Killed his wife and a couple of Hooker's Girls in Dodge City before they got onto him. But he managed to skip out. It would take an axe to do this kind of carnage, Butch. Come to think of it, there's a flyer in my saddlebags. Name's Klinger, Norbert Klinger." Rose stopped digging. "There, that ought to do it. Someone will probably want to claim the body anyhow. Lord it stinks." Gagging at the putrid effluvium, Rose bent over the body and searched it for identification with one hand while covering nose and mouth with the other.

"Well, well, Butch. Would you look at this watch. And a wad of new bills. There must be close to a hundred dollars here. Phew, eighteen carat gold and here's an inscription. 'Ben Thompson, his watch.' Humph, not the Ben Thompson we know, eh, Butch?"

Dragging the cadaver by one leg, Rose got it to the grave and rolled it in with a boot toe. The severed head came next. Earth followed, then a layer of heavy rocks to keep the coyotes at bay. Rose got up and cast around the campsite, quickly discovering sign.

"How about this, Butch? The killer is riding a horse with a barred shoe on the off front. Way I read it, we're close to twelve hours behind him." Again the piercing whistle. Mounted, Rose began to follow the killer.

"It was murder, Butch. A cold-blooded killing for a meal of burro flesh. Life's sure getting cheap, it appears."

"Get up here, you cheap slut!" roared the wild-eyed, gray-haired man as he brandished a bloody little iron-studded whip. "Get up here and take what's coming to you. Or, by God, you'll not get a cent."

"Noooo! Please, I . . . I didn't think it would hurt so bad," the disheveled, naked little blonde sobbed as she huddled more tightly in the corner of the ornately furnished room.

"You didn't *think!* Why you silly little bitch," the man shouted as he pulled the nude girl to her feet by the hair. "You never had a thought in your useless life."

Flinging the hapless young woman from the gore-smeared wall to land full length on the bed, Abner Waterford lashed out to strike her pale flesh again. Goaded on by the agonized screams, he grasped her shoulders and flopped her on her back.

Clinging to the girl's heaving torso, Abner licked his lips with relish and began to gloat. "That bastard whelp of yours will go to college if it has the brains. And when I'm through with you, you'll never have to turn another trick. You'll leave Denver to become a respected and lovely, chaste lady."

The twisted images in Abner's brain drove him to such a state of arousal that he abandoned the whip to her fleshy embrace and fumbled at his trousers.

"Ha-ha-ha!" he chortled. "When I finish with you, other men will turn from this glowing body in revulsion. You'll be true to me for the rest of your life, because you'll have no choice."

"Three dollars a shift is na' too bloody much ta' ask, mates."

Angus McRoberts shook his shaggy head and pointed with the stub end of his old briar as though he had heard dissent. Yet he knew that every man at the shabby table in the back room of the Palace Saloon on Bennet Avenue in Cripple Creek, Colorado, agreed with him. This meeting of the Western Federation of Miners and the Free

Coinage Union, comprised of three men from each organization, was unlikely to argue goals. Though, Angus had already observed, Paddy MacCarthy, sergeant-at-arms for the federation, had other priorities for achieving them.

"First we be needin' to run out all these bohunks 'n hunkies," Paddy declared.

"Don't forget the damn dagoes 'n chinks," added the federation secretary. Abe Lerner was a hulking Kentuckian who had worked Galena mines around St. Louis as a kid. Incongruous to his appearance and manner, he had learned to read, write and cypher. Unfortunately, the gentling aspects of an education somehow refused to adhere. "All the cheap labor from the silver mines is gonna put us right out of a job."

"Now that's the whole point of free coinage, boys," Alfred Briscoe spoke for the first time. "It'll bring silver back up to a realistic price and those fellows can return to work."

"Sure," Abe growled. "And in the meantime, they'll be havin' our jobs here in Cripple Crick. Well, mister, that ain't gonna happen." He glowered around the table and got a series of nervous nods.

"Gentlemen, it be our pairpus here today to form a coalition," Angus injected. "A coalition ta bring the Mine Owners Association inta line with our reasonable requests. Now, I say aye. How speak the rest a' ye?"

Ayes came from around the table and made the coalition unanimous.

"Now, fer the first order a' coalition business, I move we organize the millworkers in Colorado City. They ain't makin' hardly a livin' wage fer a twelve-hour shift an'll join up with us right handy," Abe offered. "Then we can tie a can to the tails a' these damnation furriners."

"Aye!"

"Aye!"

"Aye!"

"Aye!"

"Be ye abstainin', Mr. Briscoe?"

"Aye. No, Mr. McRoberts," Briscoe said at last. "Though I fear this is a dark day for Colorado."

C. M. Rose smelled the killer's next victim before catching sight of it. The body had been stuffed into the crotch of a cottonwood tree, the grinning head facing it from a distance wedged in the notch of two branches. With death comes a relaxing of muscle tone, including the sphincters, and the dead man had odorously voided his system. Hordes of blue-black flies swarmed over the severed head and the smooth stump of neck.

"Why?" Rose queried aloud. "What possible reason did he have?"

Ample evidence of the presence of the horse with the barred shoe showed in the soft ground under the tree. The animal, Rose had noted earlier, had pulled up a marked limp. Departing tracks gave at least a partial reason for the killing. The murderer now rode another horse and led his lame mount with the barred shoe.

"Horse stealing still gets the rope in Colorado, Butch," C. M. Rose speculated aloud. "Too bad he can't be hanged three times.

Chapter 2

Resplendent in his sartorial excellence, multimillionaire Abner Waterford sat in his opulent suite in the Brown Palace Hotel in Denver. His thick mane of white hair was neatly parted, revealing his receding hairline without any attempt at flattery. His large ears stuck out from his head and his thick, Prussian mustache of equal whiteness bristled over his small, secretive mouth. Its waggling as he spoke emphasized the long, straight aristocratic nose that adorned his lip. He disdained long sideburns, and his deep-set eyes had a hypnotic quality.

"A brace of quail to follow the soup," he dictated to the attentive waiter, looking and sounding not the least like the naked fury of the bordello two nights before. "I think braised potatoes, some carrots, a little salmon in aspic, greens, and bread to go with the roast beef. And for desert a Vienna Tort."

"Wine, sir?"

"Oh, yes, of course. Harvey's Bristol Cream with the oysters and escargot. A fine Riesling with the quail, claret from the private stock to accompany the main course. Christian Brothers brandy with desert."

"Yes, sir, it will be right up."

Abner Waterford clasped his hands together in satisfaction after the waiter departed to the kitchen five stories below. With a twenty-year lease on the suite, the mining magnate expected to relax and enjoy many more fine meals in the Brown Palace. He savored the fine Kentucky bourbon whiskey in a cut crystal glass and pressed the rim to his lips. It would take an hour to assemble and prepare his meal. He could spend the time, Abner considered, reviewing the situation on Cripple Creek.

Those damned union miners. Next thing they would have a regular rebellion going. Not that he didn't believe in safe working conditions and reasonable pay for dangerous work. It didn't take a lot of radicals and, oh God, those Molly McGuires to bring that about. Let this fledgling union get a foothold and that's what would come next. Molly McGuire terrorism right from the coal fields of Pennsylvania. He would have to arrange something with the other mine owners, the shipping company people, and the railroad.

"Another whiskey, sir?" Waterford's liveried butler asked him.

"Yes, I think I will, Jurris."

When the dinner at last arrived, mellowed by the

whiskey, Abner Waterford had to work at appearing displeased. He lifted covers and sniffed disdainfully at the plates. A sample here and there and he rendered a verdict.

"This is deplorable. Simply won't do. Send it back. The Brown Palace has the best chef in Denver and there is no excuse for this. The beef is overdone, the quail undercooked, the vegetables soggy. See that it is redone at once."

Stammering in consternation, the waiter departed, propelled along by Jurris. Waterford watched them with a smug smile. Truth was he hadn't really worked up an appetite as yet. Although willing, and more than able, to bear the expense, he would rather humiliate the chef and have the hotel pick up the check. Considering his circumstances he had little doubt how that would go. Jurris came back with a distressed expression.

"I'm sorry, sir, there are some ladies here from the Grand Army of the Republic. They insist on speaking with you."

"It's quite all right, Jurris," Waterford said through a smile. "Since my dinner appears to be delayed some while, I have time to see them."

"Er—ah, as you wish, sir."

With dignity barely restored, the butler showed in the women. They were all hats, furs, and feathers, with high-speed mouths and leather lungs. Gradually, out of their constant interruptions, Abner Waterford began to gather they had come to solicit funding for an orphanage.

"The poor little dears have nowhere else to go.

Some of them, not over ten, we've found living naked in caves," one dowager bemoaned.

"Others, barely older if at all, were caught up in the commerce of sin, selling their young bodies for a few coins to the sort of depraved beasts who fancy little girls or boys, in order to purchase food and shelter," wailed a skinny woman with large liver spots on her hands and neck.

"And you good ladies propose to establish an asylum for these waifs?" Waterford managed to inject.

"Absolutely," a buxom woman who introduced herself as Abigale assured him.

Waterford summoned Jurris and asked for his book of checks. When the butler brought it, the mining potentate made elaborate gestures while opening it and selecting a steel-nib pen. He wrote in a large, round copperplate, and the women came close to swooning as those closest read the figures.

"T-two hun-hundred thousand dollars!" Abigale shrieked. "Oh, Mr. Waterford, we knew you to be a generous man, but, oh, sir, this is magnificent. We can have our orphanage opened within a week with so gracious a donation."

"Fine," Waterford answered, his mind filled with visions of tender, silken young female flesh. "And I'll be around from time to time to inspect."

Below in the kitchens, Henri Flobert, the *chef de cuisine* employed by the Browns, prepared to personally take the remade dinner up to their most particular and demanding patron. Sweating and humiliated, he hefted the huge tray onto a service cart and started for the door.

"Henri," the pastery chef commiserated with him, "you should not debase yourself by going in person to Monsieur Waterford. It is beneath your dignity."

"Not to worry, Gilbert. Thees time I piss in zee bastard's zoup."

C. M. Rose held the long red tail hair in a gloved hand and studied the ground around the campsite. The killer had rubbed down both horses. One of them obviously a sorrel or strawberry roan. For the first time Rose found a splash mark where one horse urinated. It formed a long crater, which indicated a mare. Other tracks around the camp suggested that the killer had a club right foot; the depth of the impressions gave a rough estimate of his size as around six feet tall and close to two hundred pounds. The wet earth at the pee spot and warmth in the ground around the fire ring clearly indicated that the distance between them was lessening. They were nearing Denver, Colorado, and Rose had no doubt the killer would head that way. If this was indeed Norbert Klinger, Rose felt fairly sure of recognizing him.

"They had it in the paper, Butch," Rose said to the gold-eyed wolf dog, "that this Klinger was a woodcutter by trade. From what we've seen, he's mighty handy with that axe. And I can see from those oblong marks by his footprints that when he's tired, he uses it for a cane. We can't be more than twenty miles from Denver, Butch. Odds say we'll find him there."

Violence had become a too-regular part of the mine strike in Cripple Creek. Abner Waterford, as a principal mine owner, had been invited to a meeting of the newly formed Cripple Creek Citizen's Alliance. Shop owners, saloon keepers, and a number of local residents organized the alliance to find an effective means of dealing with the strikers. What Abner had heard so far didn't please him.

"I say they're nothing but ignorant clods," the portly haberdasher, Lem Biel snarled. "First they throw sticks of dynamite at the mine offices and the front gates. What next? We have to meet force with force."

"You gonna dynamite those shacks they live in, Lem?" Abner asked dryly.

"Don't be ridic'lus, Abner," Lem countered, flushing. "I mean we need people to protect our property. No tellin' what these Irish and bohunks might take a mind to do."

"Lem's right, Abner," Doc Silver, a saloon owner injected. "Some of them had a meeting at my saloon couple of nights ago to discuss electin' leaders. Split a solid damn oak table with one blow of a miner's pick, that O'Malley feller did.

What law we've got in this town's cowed by them. It's time we take action."

"I propose," Cynthia Gleason, the only woman present put in, "that we hire some contract lawmen. Like that handsome William Masterson."

"Bat Masterson wouldn't come to Cripple Creek," the town's leading grocer stated. "I hear he's fixin' to leave Denver and take a spell back East. New York City, of all places."

"New York City!" several present chorused. "There's something wrong with that boy."

"We have to go at this at a better pace," Abner insisted. "Runaway talk about hiring gunman can get us more grief than we already have."

"I agree with Lem and Miz Gleason. If we don't shut them down, those strikers are gonna take what they want whenever they want to," another merchant announced.

"Well now," Lem Biel summed up. "It appears we have a solid course of action outlined. I happen to have the name of just the man to head up this police force. Sam Steele. Shall we vote on it?"

"Lem, I'm warning you. Miners are people, just like us. If you go importing gunfighters, especially a man with a reputation like Steele carries, we're going to be the losers. I won't have anything to do with such a scheme," Abner Waterford announced.

"You're gonna vote no?" Lem inquired.

"I'm not voting at all. I'm leaving this meeting. If the rest of you are half as smart as I think you are, you'll do the same." So stating, Abner Waterford rose and stalked out of the room.

Caleb Sturgis had lived in Poverty Gulch for as long as he had been in Cripple Creek. Not that at times he couldn't afford far more luxurious accommodations. He *preferred* living there with his family of seven children and a caring wife. He and Abner Waterford went back a long ways. Together they'd prospected the Colorado goldfields from Wagonwheel Gap to Battle Mountain, and neither was the sort to forget an old friend. Their declining years made no difference. Caleb, at sixty, remained vigorous — he had sired his youngest boy, Nathan Hale Sturgis, at fifty-one — despite a debilitating ongoing infection in his left leg. For short spells, it would put him abed. He was having one such relapse when Abner visited him directly after leaving the Citizen's Alliance meeting.

"You're lookin' like you're gonna thunder and rain all over everyone, Abe," Caleb observed.

He sat up in bed, his nine-year-old son beside him. The boy's raggedy trousers had been cut short at a tear in one leg, and Caleb rested one hand on the youngster's bare thigh. His bright blue eyes twinkled at the prospect of the long visit with his friend. Abner Waterford didn't come as often as in earlier years. His stormy expression troubled Caleb Sturgis.

"It's those damned fools in town," Abner growled.

Sturgis patted the redheaded boy's leg. "You go find James Monroe and Betsy Ross, Nathan. Tell 'em that just because school is out of session it doesn't interfere with their doin' the chores." Caleb had named all his children after heroes and heroines of the American Revolution.

"Yes, sir," Nathan chirped. He bounded from the bed and padded barefoot from the room.

"What is it this time?"

Before he made answer, Abner fished into an inside coat pocket and withdrew his large, fat wallet. From it he extracted a thick sheaf of bills, rolled them and stuck them under the sick man's mattress. "Considerin' what those boneheads in town have done, you may have use of that. Call it a loan. Just a grub stake for until you get better and strike it rich again. But I want you to swear you'll not tell anyone where the money came from."

"I'll agree to that, Abner, but what *is it* that the townsfolk have done?"

"They got them a committee, Caleb. Cripple Creek Citizen's Alliance they call it. And they went and voted today to bring in gunfighters to break this strike and restore what they call 'order.' "

"Hired guns in Cripple Creek?" Caleb said lamely.

"Yes, by damnit. I walked out, but little good that did. We're going to see blood in the streets and businesses shut down because of this crazy idea. I don't agree with the miners' wage demands, but I do approve of the safety measures they insist on. I happen to *like* the men who work for me. They're not 'cattle' to be herded around by rings in their noses, like some hold. Worst of it is, those nervous Nellies picked Sam Steele to be head of the new Safety Committee."

Caleb and Abner talked on at length about affairs in Cripple Creek, and of Waterford's interests in Denver. At last, the handsome, gray-haired man rose and took his leave. Matilda Biel, Caleb's wife, entered in a rush. She pushed at stray wisps of graying yellow hair that had escaped her bun and then wrung her hands.

"I don't like that man. I'm sorry, Caleb, but I have to speak my mind. He gives me the creepies when he looks at me or one of our daughters."

Caleb released a heavy sigh. "I have to own it's true; Abner Waterford hates women. Though I allow as how he has good enough reasons for his opinion. Still, I reckon that Abner's probably the most knowledgeable man in the goldfields and dead loyal to his friends."

"What of those horrible stories whispered about him around town?" Matilda prompted.

"Enough of that, Tilly," Caleb returned roughly. "I've no intention of hearing my own wife speak ill of my best friend. Nor will I have her remark on the goings-on in the bordellos. Wherever does a respectable woman hear such things?"

Matilda answered him with a sniff. She was not about to rat on her friends and be ordered not to associate with them anymore. Miss all that juicy gossip? Not likely. "I must say that it is common knowledge."

"Since when have you been *common*, woman?"

Caleb growled.

Matilda fled the room, her last argument in disarray.

Norbert Klinger lay flat on his belly at the verge of the creek bank a mile outside Denver. He parted the tall grass with thick, calloused fingers and peered at the naked boys splashing in the clear, cold water. How they could stand it, he didn't know. Sunlight sparkled off their wet bodies and Norbert found himself breathing hard, his lips suddenly dry and his heart pounding faster. A familiar and hated tingling radiated from his loins. He ran his tongue around his parched lips and a soft groan escaped him when the lads climbed from the water. Fervently, urgently, he began to pray.

All but one began to dress. "Aren'tcha comin' Tommy?" a black-haired youngster inquired.

"Naw. I did my chores before I left for the crick. I wanna lay on this rock and let the sun dry me," the towheaded Tommy Walsh replied.

It took the boys only moments to finish their tasks. They started off barefoot along a pathway. One of them whistled off-key. Left behind, Tommy sprawled on a large, flat, gray rock. The sun tingled on his skin and the gentle breeze seemed to caress him. Eyes closed, the solar orb creating a reddish curtain, his mind began to wander. Suddenly a footfall crunched on the creek bank gravel and alerted Tommy to danger.

He opened his eyes to see a blur of gleaming metal descending. Then light exploded painfully into blackness and all sensations left him.

"You're filth," Norbert Klinger wailed as he brought his axe into contact with silken, sun-browned flesh and decapitated little Tommy Walsh.

Chapter 3

Business went on as usual in Denver. From the activity, one would never know that strikes had been called at the mines in Cripple Creek and Colorado City. The streets bustled with pedestrian traffic while carts and wagons, horses and mules set them scurrying for the boardwalks when they incautiously ventured into the rutted lanes. C. M. Rose hit Denver at four-thirty in the afternoon without catching up to the quarry. The tragic scene on the creek bank had sickened and angered the bounty hunter. The corpse of the little boy had been carefully dressed and lay across Lucifer's flanks, behind the saddle. A cloth had been used to conceal the head. Eyes burning with rage, Rose sought out any red horse, or the cross-barred cripple. A sorry task awaited and C. M. Rose didn't relish it. A portly sergeant in uniform sat at the tall desk in the lobby of the police station when Rose entered.

"Yes, what can I do for you, sir?" he inquired in a bored tone.

The raspy voice answered him. "I want to report a murder. A small boy. He—he had his head cut off. I think I know who is responsible and I need help finding him. I've a wanted poster on him and intend to collect the reward."

"Bounty hunter, eh? Ye'r a might young for that, ain'cha? 'Sides, we don't take too warmly to your type around Denver."

"I have a lawful warrant and a badge authorizing me to bring in certain criminals," C. M. Rose returned.

"Do ye now? An' what's yer name?" the sergeant pressed.

"C. M. Rose," came the reply.

"Ummmmm. Never heard of that one before. Mayhap ye've not run afoul of the law, like so many of yer callin'."

"I'm after an axe murderer, sergeant. Norbert Klinger. Here's a warrant from Trail City and a reward poster from Dodge City. I've followed Klinger here and I've come to let you know. Also to ask for assistance in my search. I have the body of a boy about eleven out on my horse. His head is in my saddlebag. He has been beheaded with an axe or a mighty big knife."

"Know who he is?" the sergeant demanded.

"No. I do not," Rose replied.

"Ed, you come along." The sergeant summoned an officer. "We'll go take a look. Then, if all's as ye say, Mr. Rose, we'll send Ed along with you to find your axe killer."

Outside, C. M. Rose exposed the head and torso of the boy. Ed Newman gagged and paled. His handsome features writhed with revulsion. The sergeant turned white and shook his head in sorrow and confusion. "That's Peter Walsh's boy, Tommy. Awh, Mary an' all the saints, how'm I gonna tell him? The Walsh is a night duty officer," he explained to Rose, "on our department. By Jasas, it'll be hard on him to learn of this. There's a swimmin' hole on the creek, about a mile outta town. Is it there that ye found him?"

"Yes," Rose answered tightly.

"Alone?"

"He was then. I saw sign of some five other boys around the area, also the clubfooted prints of Klinger's boots."

"What was his condition, ah, besides havin' . . . havin' his head cut off?" the sergeant asked.

"He was naked as a jaybird," the raspy voice replied.

"Any sign of, ah, you know, irregularities?" the sergeant asked, embarrassed.

"None," Rose answered him.

"What kind of dirty bastard would do a thing like this?" the sergeant growled, putting words to Rose's thoughts. "Ed, ye'll accompany Mr. C. M. Rose on a round of the town. Look for this strawberry roan an' find the man responsible for this terrible crime. Oh, ah, ye'll still be able to claim your reward, Mr. Rose. Meanwhile, I'd better see Father Vincent and we'll go together to inform poor Peter."

With Rose leading, Ed began to sense some sort of irregularity. The bounty hunter certainly had a lively movement to hips and legs. If he didn't know better, Ed thought, he'd suspect the fellow's gender. After two blocks it became too compelling not to ask.

"By the way, what does the C. M. stand for?" Patrolman Ed Newman inquired.

"Charity Moira," Rose responded sweetly.

Confronted with the accuracy of his suspicions, Ed's jaw sagged. "My God, you *are* a woman."

"Of course. I always have been. Shall we continue?"

"Yes. But, ah, I think I should take the lead. After all, Miss Charity, it is my town."

"Oh, I'm sure that's the only reason, Ed," Charity responded.

Ed hitched his gun belt and set off in the lead, much to Charity's amused disgust. Men. All alike. The flower of womanhood must be protected from life's harsher realities. She wondered if Ed would step in the way of a bullet in a mistaken belief that he must protect her. On Halliday Street, in front of a notorious crib operated by a pair of semi-retired hookers, they spotted a strawberry roan. Charity hurried to inspect the hoofs.

"I'd, ah, exercise a bit more caution, Miss

Charity," Ed spoke softly.

Charity ignored him and lifted each hoof in turn. She nodded, satisfied. "It's his horse, all right. One he took from a man he killed. The one with the crossbar will probably be at the livery, or a vet's. It came up lame some time back. Well, let's go in. *Claon,* Butch," she spoke to the wolf dog.

Butch immediately went to heel. Ed Newman shook his head dubiously. With the policeman well in the lead, Charity crossed the wide boardwalk and placed her ear to the door. Hearing moans, she backed up and kicked the door.

She rebounded instantly, then drew her right-hand Bisley and shot the lock. This time the door yielded. Reacting to the shot, Newman bounded forward and tried to take over again. Charity pushed him aside and entered a shabby parlor. Although still daylight, blinds had been pulled over the windows to either side of the doorway. It added a gloomy quality to the shabbiness of the sitting room. A partly filled whiskey bottle, three empty beer bottles, and some glasses adorned a low table near the well-worn sofa. Charity directed her attention to the closed portal at the back of the room. Behind it, at least two women screamed lustily.

Charity crossed the room and reached for the latch. Before she grasped it, the door burst open to reveal a naked man with an axe in hand. Without hesitation, he charged into the room and knocked Charity to the floor in the process.

Charity rolled frantically, feeling a tug against her buttock as the axe head buried itself in the flooring.

"Sodom and Gomorrah! Satan walking the land!" the naked axe man shouted at them.

Twisting around violently, Charity cocked the Bisley and leveled the muzzle between the maddened, glaring eyes of the killer, who struggled to free the axe head. For a frozen instant they stared at each other, then Klinger again heaved on the axe, the head of which was firmly wedged between two boards. A quick look around showed Ed Newman immobile in the doorway. Knowing she'd have to kill Klinger to stop him, Charity applied pressure to the trigger.

Recovered from his paralysis of surprise, officer Newman exploded through the parlor and took Klinger down and through the bedroom door in a flying tackle. In that same moment, the hammer fell on Charity's Bisley. The slug blew plaster off the wall and became a contributing factor to the caterwauling of the naked whores. Finding himself no match for the strength of the madman, Ed Newman bellowed for help.

Charity charged into the fray. Her Bisley gripped tightly, she swung the four and three-quarter-inch barrel at the shaggy black head. With a death grip on the lawman's throat, Klinger took the Colt to the back of his head with hardly a flinch. Charity blinked, then wound up to deliver a second, devastating blow.

Far from finishing him, it only caused the killer to release his grip and turn on her.

Nimbly, Charity sidestepped so that her bullet would not go through Klinger's thick body and kill Newman. She had no sooner set herself when she got knocked sprawling by Klinger and slammed into the huddled hookers. With that minor annoyance taken care of, Klinger again turned on Newman. The agile lawman landed a solid right cross to the mad man's jaw. The axe murderer merely shook his head, blinked and grabbed for the lawman. Newman panicked.

Watching the action, Charity managed to get untangled from the human mess. Holding the Bisley by its stallion neck grip, she took a powerful swing. It slammed the Colt's cylinder against the killer's temple. This time, Klinger's glittering black eyes rolled up and he collapsed. Still shaken, Ed Newman was at last able to put manacles on him.

"He's a regular fury," Ed spoke up, panting. "It's a good thing I came along."

"If you hadn't been along, I would have been able to shoot him between the eyes instead of having him carted out of danger and cause us more grief," Charity snapped, the adrenaline still charging her with anger. She turned to the prostitutes. "Get his pants on so we can take him to jail."

"Oh, but, *look* at us. Uh, no, don't look at us!" one wailed.

"Yes. We have to make ourselves decent first."

Suddenly Charity's butt began to sting and she lost all patience. "Sister, you haven't been decent in years. Get your asses in gear and get this man dressed. You can tend to yourselves later."

"B-b-but in front of two men," the second hooker shrieked.

Ed Newman noticed the cause of Charity's stinging sensation and spoke rapidly. "Charity, you — ah — you're bleeding from the, ah, posterior region."

Struck silent by this revelation the soiled doves realized for the first time that the *gunman* was a lady, and they were totally confused. Charity decided to tend to her immediate problem and get a look at her wound. After several attempts she ceased twisting and turning in exasperation.

"I'll be happy to help you with a thorough examination," Ed Newman offered eagerly.

"I'm sure you would," Charity replied heatedly, rightly suspecting an ulterior motive. "For the time being, I'll drape myself with a towel and go to a doctor when we've finished here."

In keeping with her words, she draped a towel through her gun belt and rigged it diaper fashion. It looked ludicrous and Ed Newman had to stifle a snicker at the image it presented. Charity's icy green stare helped him in that endeavor. Moving briskly he hurried off to a "call box" to summon the Black Maria. As he departed he cast reluctant, uncertain glances at Charity, left with the violent prisoner in her care.

Wind swept down the narrow, rutted main street of the new boom town of Creede, Colorado. A brisk mountain shower had recently combined with the urine of hundreds of horses to turn the thoroughfare into a quagmire. It stank wretchedly. A few scruffy dogs haunted the shadows. Business establishments seemed to be doing rather well, despite the midday hour. A casual observer would never guess that most of the residents of Creede were off working their claims, or laboring for those who found gold deep in half a dozen mines. The miners' strike had not reached Creede. One establishment, a saloon, appeared to be the only exception to this busy prospect.

Named for its owner, the Ford Exchange, it occupied a position in the middle of one block. Inside, the proprietor, a tall man with broad, thick shoulders, shiny black hair, and flourishing mustache stood behind the bar. Whether true or not, Bob Ford had become notorious as the man who shot Jesse James. Now he sought anonymity and protection from would-be avengers in the life of a mild-mannered saloon keeper.

Much to Bob's regret, it didn't always work that way. At the moment, Ford found himself confronted by four hardcases with the clout to have ordered his customers from the premises. One of them was as infamous a frontier figure as himself. Soapy Smith, the self-appointed law in Creede, frequently supplemented his income from fines and the stipend paid by the city fathers by selling "protection" to the merchants. He had tried to compel Bob Ford to cough up money in the past, only to be daunted by the man's reputation. Recently Soapy had learned that public opinion had been shifting.

Flamboyant articles in the eastern press and the dime novels had turned the James Boys into latter-day Robin Hoods. The Fords, Bob and Charlie, had been cast in the role of villains. Even the inhabitants of the frontier, who should know better, had taken to this new version. As a result, Soapy decided to try again.

"This is a fine establishment," Soapy said expansively. "It would be a shame if it were to catch fire. The volunteer fire department is financed in, ah, part by funds from the assurance money collected from merchants. What if the strike comes to Creede? Surely, out of work miners with nagging wives and hungry brats at home could do considerable damage to a place if their tempers flared. Then there's bunko artists and crooked gamblers, fireship girls, all of whom could give your place a terrible reputation by what they took from or gave to your customers."

"Damn you, Soapy, you've been after me since I opened the door. Each time you make the story a little worse," Bob Ford growled. "It it weren't for these three, ah, deputies of yours, I've a mind to heave you out on the boardwalk."

Soapy raised an admionitory hand. "Harsh words, Bob Ford. Especially coming from the man who shot Jesse James in the back."

Anger made a beet of Ford's face. "That story's a lot of cow chips, and you know it."

"All the same, there's lots who believe it. That alone's enough to cost you business. I think you really ought to reconsider."

Silence held in the saloon while Bob Ford let go his steam. An expression of bitterness and chagrin twisted his face. He started to speak, thought better of it, and held his peace. Grinning, Soapy Smith added another brick to the load.

"These, ah, assessments have been a ritual of long standing. Even before there was a Creede, folks around offered me good money to protect them."

Ford studied the faces of the four determined and united men. "Damn. Awh, dammit. I suppose at this point I haven't any other choice. How much is it going to be?"

Soapy Smith arranged his features into a mask of contemplation. "Considerin' I've extended you protection for the past two months without charge, some sort of adjustment needs to be made. Say . . . fifty a week."

"Fifty dollars!" Bob Ford shouted. "I can't possibly . . . That's outrageous."

"Fifty a week is cheap, compared to having the place burn down or seeing it turned into a low dive that only the least desirable patron would crawl in here. Think that over."

"I have. And . . . I . . . How long do I have to

get it together for you?"

"Tomorrow morning will be just fine," Soapy Smith said through a beatific smile.

Chapter 4

Barefoot youngsters ran laughing and shouting behind the glossy black wagon with the bold silver letters on the side, Police. A bell clanged constantly. Charity Rose rode beside an officer on a small rear platform. She clung to a curved iron rail for support. When they reached the police station, she dismounted and saw to Klinger's removal from "Maria."

"We'll take him in this way, Miss Charity," Ed Newman explained. "First he'll be booked, then stripped and thoroughly searched. Then it's off to a cell. Other parties having a prior claim on him will be notified. Chances are we'll lose jurisdiction over him and he'll hang somewhere else. If I had my own way, I'd like to kill him outright for what he did to little Tommy Walsh."

"So would I," Charity agreed through clinched teeth.

"Why don't you go on around to the desk sergeant and process the papers for your reward. They'll go forward with the notification of our having him in custody."

"I think I will," Charity readily agreed.

She walked to the front of the building with Butch tagging at her heels. When she entered, the desk sergeant looked up. "So ye brought him in, did ye? That's a fine piece of work. We'll get the papers taken care of for yer reward and then all we have to do is wait. Uh, say, ye've been nicked is it? A bit of a hurt from baggin' this devil?"

"Yes, it is, sergeant," Charity agreed.

"O'Toole, get yerself off to Doc McDade's. Have him come on the run, will ye?"

"Right, sergeant," Sean O'Toole responded as he rose, eyeing the bloodstained towel and the thought-provoking location of the wound.

"Now, as I was sayin'," the sergeant said to Charity. "Once the documents are out of the way, all we do is wait. If no one wants to stand the expense of transporting him back for trial and a hanging, then we inherit him. In that case, you'll have to remain here for the trial. Anyway, here's paper for ye to write yer report on."

Charity set about the task, using a neat, precise script. The words flowed onto paper. She had barely concluded when the doctor arrived. Rather than the portly, middle-aged man with waggling goatee, she looked up to see quite the sexiest male she had ever met.

"You're Mr. Rose?" the medico boomed heartily. "Dr. Marcus McDade. Take down your pants."

Charity's heart thundered and her belly began to melt at the first sound of his rich baritone voice. "I really think I'd like some privacy for that. You see, I'm a lady," Charity answered him quietly.

"I don't believe it!" Marcus McDade exploded. "You can't be. A lady gunfighter and bounty hunter. No."

Stung by his attitude, and a bit chagrined at the realization that it was her own insistence on the masculine disguise that had misled him, Charity could only fume silently. In moments the seriousness of her situation overcame her pique.

"Doctor," she said sharply. "No matter my gender; the fact remains that I have been bleeding for some time and I still am, as Sergeant Mahoney observed. Please, can we go to your office and get treatment for my wound?"

"Ah . . . certainly. I'm sorry. I forgot myself in my sudden discovery. Please come along. I'll lead the way," Dr. McDade offered in gentlemanly fashion.

Her temper not fully in check, Charity snapped, "Do men always feel compelled to lead women around? I just finished fighting with a crazed axe murderer. Surely that should qualify me to walk together with you as an equal."

"Whoa! I didn't want to imply I'd make you keep a respectable three paces behind me. Considering your blood loss, it might be necessary to assist you."

"Thank you, doctor. I think I can do without assistance."

After they departed, Sergeant Mahoney and Patrolman O'Toole exchanged significant glances. "Looks like the Doc's got himself a wildcat this time," Mahoney observed.

Still fuming, Charity accompanied Dr. McDade to his office, three doors down Larimer Street from the police station. They entered the building and the physician directed her to an inner room. There he set down his medical bag and turned to her.

"Drop your drawers and bend over my desk there," Dr. McDade demanded.

"I'll do nothing of the kind," Charity snapped. "Have you so quickly forgotten my gender?"

Marcus McDade raised an eyebrow. "Hardly," he breathed huskily. "In light of it, I think it wise if you take your trousers all the way off before you bend over the desk."

All of the initial anger engendered by the doctor's reaction at the discovery of her gender had rekindled. The fury colored her heated words. "Why in hell should I do that when a man wouldn't?" she demanded.

"To be washed and repaired, of course," Dr. McDade replied reasonably. "Unless you propose to walk around Denver with your delightful posterior sticking out of a bloody pair of jeans."

"Oh!" Charity squeaked, off balance. "Well, in that case, I must bow to your judgment, doctor. I have a clean pair in my bedroll."

"Good. I'll bring them to you when I've finished. Where are your belongings located?"

"At the police station, tied on my saddle. It's on the black horse at the tie rail."

"Excellent. Now, there's a gown behind that screen. If you'll just divest yourself of those bloody rags, we can commence caring for your wound."

Meekly, Charity started for the white cotton cloth screen, stretched over a metal frame. She had to remove her boots first, only to discover a pool of blood in one. Then she slid out of the broadcloth trousers, wincing at the brief, sharp twinges of pain her movement generated. She tied the hospital gown in place and stepped out before the young man.

"Ah, there we are. If you'll just hoist that and bend over, I can begin," Dr. McDade said in cool, clinical tones.

"What's wrong with that bed over there?" Charity complained.

"My surgical table? Well, it's too high for one; and you can't lay on it properly because of the position of the wound. Bend, please? And put your left foot in that large bowl to catch the runoff."

Despite flaming-faced humiliation, Charity complied. A moment later she decided she liked the deft, probing feel of the doctor's hands as he sluiced cool water over her hot bottom and leg. "Ummmm. It's starting to throb," she advised him.

"That's to be expected. The shock to the nerves is wearing off. Now the alcohol."

All the fires of hell couldn't be worse, Charity thought, as the stinging liquid washed over her open wound. Damn this good-looking young McDade. He must be deliberately rough in applying it to get even. Then came the needle.

Sweat beaded Charity's forehead as she hung on to the desk edges with whitened knuckles. Gritting her teeth against any sound, she tried not to flinch while the doctor took stitch after stitch in the tender skin of her buttock. Long before the final suture, her flesh shrank from the doctor's touch as from a hot iron.

"That's certainly no way to treat a lady. Couldn't you have given me something for the pain?"

"Not really," Marcus replied to the latter remark first. "Besides, I wasn't aware ladies went about in male garb, picking fights with men in a bordello and collecting bounties."

"Do you use the power of your position to pat the fanny of every female patient, doctor?" Charity retaliated.

With an impatient snort, Dr. McDade stalked off to fetch her bedroll. Charity took time to study the office. It had a distinctly masculine air to it. Heavy leather furniture, a potbellied stove, empty and ignored in the warm weather, a large, squarish desk — over which she leaned — and a small rolltop against one wall completed the furniture. She had noted a coat tree and another desk in the outer office, or waiting room. Shiny brass lamps sat in strategic places. Engravings and pencil sketches of wild game adorned the walls. There was a pleasant hint of pipe tobacco. Taken together, with his divine good looks, Charity considered that, given other circumstances, the doctor was a person with whom she would like to be better acquainted. A commotion from outside attracted her attention.

Charity hurried through the waiting room to peek out a window. On the way she recalled that the bedroll, along with her other gear, was being guarded by both Butch and Lucifer. One look at the street told it all. Charity snatched up a folded blanket, wrapped it around her waist and rushed out onto the boardwalk. The chill, slimy texture of a huge gobbet of discarded chewing tobacco reminded her that she was barefoot. A shudder of disgust passed over her as she hurried to where Butch had Dr. McDade cornered.

One leg of the doctor's trousers was shredded, and red streaks showed where fangs had scraped flesh. Lucifer stamped about, ears plastered back, his desire to use hoofs and teeth against the intruder inhibited by tied-off reins. An amused crowd had been drawn by the growls, whinnies, and human shouts of alarm. In all the confusion, Charity made poor choice of her words.

"*Matti cu*, Butch. *Fan*," she said hurriedly, calling him a good dog in Gaelic and ordering him to hold.

Quickly she set to soothing Lucifer. His neck came unarched and the strain on the reins relaxed. Charity reached for the bedroll with one hand while she held the blanket in place with the other. Embarrassed at the scene, Charity started a headlong charge for the doctor's door.

"Hey, you forgot the doctor," one of the crowd hollered.

Realizing her mistake, Charity recalled her dog. "*Amach*, Butch, *amach*."

Released, the terrified Dr. McDade started after her, now as angry as she had been earlier. Back in the office, Charity cut off his accusations that she had deliberately set him up by pointing out the scrape marks on his calf.

"I'll be happy to clean and disinfect those, if you like. To, ah, make amends for what my dog did?" she ended sweetly. Long lashes fluttering over deep sea-green eyes did much to restore the doctor's humor.

"All right, if you wish. The alcohol is in the cabinet over there. The white one with the glass door."

Charity found it there, right next to the Absorbine Sr., which he no doubt used on his equine patients. "I'll get changed first, if it's all right," she called over one shoulder.

"Go ahead, I can wait," Marcus replied a bit testily.

Charity quickly slid into her fresh trousers, fitted wool socks, then drained and wiped dry her boot. Back in suitable dress, she buckled the Lawrence rig over the new pants, adjusted the hang of the holsters, and rerolled her blankets.

"I'm ready if you are, " she said brightly from

the cabinet. "Face the back of that chair and prop your knee on it."

He complied as she crossed the room to him, his back to her. With a pair of shears she trimmed the pantleg away from the fang marks. Then, in a fleeting moment before the smell reached his nostrils, she drenched the wound with horse liniment. Fire exploded in Marcus McDade's leg the same instant he recognized the Absorbine Sr. Charity had already made her hasty exit, which left the young doctor dancing around the room and manfully trying to refrain from swearing at her. Or whimpering.

Armed with pick handles, members of the Western Miners Union, under the leadership of Angus McRoberts and Abe Larner, marched on the stope of the Holy Moses Silver and Amethyst Mine on the outskirts of Creede. The union men weren't from Creede. They had been imported from Denver and the stalled mines at Cripple Creek. A few local toughs had been thrown in for good measure. The cause of the invasion was the loyalty of the local miners for their employers.

"Those Creede miners are workin' a ten hour shift for three dollars," Angus had belabored the unionists before departure for Creede. "Instead of strikin' with us to keep the three dollars for an eight hour shift, or starvin' as other silver miners are where the mine owners aren't payin' because there ain't no amethyst to cover expenses, they're takin' their Judas money and betrayin' our cause. It's time we made them know that what they are doin' is bloody treason!"

The Holy Moses didn't own a company store or company housing, so the employees felt they had an adequate income. They also had work when others didn't. So far they had rebuked every attempt at organizing. When the mob of not-so-gentle organizers reached Creede early in the morning and climbed to the crest of the hill, a crew of company police appeared from the mine office to block the union men from access to the mine.

"Capitalist lackeys!" Abe Larner shouted.

"Who let you boys outta what prison?" another striking miner demanded.

The hired gunmen stood their ground while the shrill steam whistle signaled time for the first shift. Those at the rear of the union formation saw the local miners spilling from their homes and starting up the hill. They quickly passed the word. Low-hanging clouds swallowed the mountaintops around and smeared dampness on the faces of everyone outside. From a window of the office, the mine manager watched the angry crowd below.

"Scab, scab, dirty scab," the unionists began to chant as the Holy Moses miners filed past to their work.

Several menaced the non-union men with their pick handles. Heads forward, lunch buckets tucked under arms, the workers ignored the threats and taunts. To Angus McRoberts it began to look like a Mexican standoff. Neither side would give an inch and no one would initiate any violence. Picket signs began to be brandished more like weapons than advertisements of sentiment. Then one of the picketers made a side-arm throw of his hickory handle.

It struck a Holy Moses miner in the leg with the sound of a pistol shot. Shrieking in pain, the miner fell to the ground, his limb broken. Quick as a striking timber rattler, Sam Steele's hand flashed and the assailant dropped dead. Cries of alarm and angry mutters rose among the unionists. In the same instant, all along the line of shootists, six-guns came out and leveled on the unionists. Here and there a rifle or shotgun added greater threat.

"Ye murderin' bastid, we saw which one of you did it. We'll be fixin' yer stew far ye," Paddy Flarity bellowed, tears streaming from his eyes.

For a moment it looked as though there would be an unfair battle between hickory clubs and guns. The unionists took determined steps toward the unarmed miners. The hired guns raised their weapons.

"Easy lads, take it easy," Angus McRoberts urged quietly as he stepped into the breach created by the killing. "There'll be plenty of time for that."

"Aye," one hard-faced miner allowed. "First there's the wake to attend to, then Brandon Gallagher's funeral. Then we'll be comin' to take care o' the likes o' these."

"That's it. That's the spirit," Angus encouraged,

seizing the concept. "We've our first martyr, lads, Gather a'roond and lift him hee. We'll carry him with solemn dignity and mourn him among our own. But bear in mind," Angus went on, his voice rising as he addressed the non-striking miners and the gunmen who guarded the Holy Moses. "They days o' yer evil are numbered, and the time's comin' when ye'll pay for your wickedness."

Chapter 5

Flocks of starlings and pigeons clouded the sky when the bell in a tall, stone clock tower struck the hour of four in the afternoon. Charity Rose, once more restored in her garb as a young man, entered the Windsor Hotel on Larimer Street and engaged a room. Once settled in, she set out to purchase suitable town clothing, a pressing need because the tight-fitting riding breeches had begun chafing against her sutures. At the first ladies wear she located, her appearance and request generated a startled reponse.

"Why, I'll do nothing of the sort!" the indignant proprietress responded. "Aiding a nice young man like you to engage in some fanciful perversion would be like committing a crime."

Patiently, Charity explained her circumstances and convinced the woman that she was indeed female. Soon she luxuriated in the scintillating pleasures of baggy underdrawers and sibilantly whispering skirts. Indulging her whim of the moment, she prolonged her try-ons and choices, sensually absorbing a feminine rebirth in the variety of garments. The dress she chose at last was an elegant, emerald green affair that set off her auburn hair and green eyes. It seemed to intensify her sun-bronzed face and draw attention to her fine-boned figure. Her pampering served another purpose.

Still miffed at Dr. McDade's lack of sympathy, or of arousal to her artfully presented bare charms, she selected a second frock, one with a huge bow at the rear that emphasized her delightfully prominent derrier. Dressed in this, her other gown in a clothes box, she marched out into the street. Armed with a parasol and high-button shoes, Charity hiked back toward Halliday Street and, on a whim, entered another women's store.

One glance at the stock and her experience with the jades of the trail informed Charity that this establishment was frequented almost exclusively by soiled doves. Ideas began to abound in her copper-topped head and a mischievous smile lighted her face as she browsed over the stock.

"These are lovely," she stated to the shop owner, displaying a sheer pair of black silk panties. Such brief garments she knew were worn exclusively by women of ill repute.

"They are nice," the middle-aged former hooker who ran the shop allowed, studying her customer. "But are they really *you,* dearie?"

"Ooh, I think they are. At least for what I have in mind. You see, I have this husband who has been stricken with a terrible lack of interest of late," she invented, with the golden, curly locks, impudent smile, and handsome features of Dr. Marcus McDade in mind. "I intend to cure this malady right fast."

A rich, contralto chuckle emanated from the former bawd's long, still unwrinkled throat. "Oh, you sound quite devilish when you say that. Am I right in thinking that he is somewhat older and that what he used to do all night now takes him all night to do?"

"Not exactly," Charity replied.

"Surely with a beauty like you around he's no need to sew wild oats?"

"Not in the least. I'm sure of that because he doesn't even . . . even . . ."

"Ah! He doesn't plow the ground he has, eh? Well then, what you need is something to draw him back into the field. What about this marvelous, frilly little thing?"

She showed Charity a lovely, sheer green silk nightgown. At first the young bounty hunter doubted it would be suitable. Then the image blossomed behind her eyes of a gaping Marcus McDade and her scornful lack of interest when he became most aroused. *That* would assure a championship revenge. Without further hesitation she bought it and left with gleeful anticipation.

An unnatural stillness reigned over the normally bustling town of Creede, Colorado. Mine slopes stood silent, except for the occasional whistle for a cage lift as the small force of non-union miners went about their business. Exhausted at the end of ten hour shifts, they were nowhere in evidence around the camp. The union miners, long since bereft of funds, could no longer afford to avail themselves of the local saloons. Notable exceptions to this were their organizers.

"Angus, dammit, it's done!" Abe Larner insisted as they huddled over their drinks at the end of the bar in the Ford Exchange. "I've sent for Al Horsley a month back and that's the end of it."

"And I be tellin' ye I'll have no part o' it, laddie." Angus pounded the mahogany to emphasize his words. Several heads turned, yet Angus went on, determined to make his point.

"Albert E. Horsley is wanted fer the murder o' dozens o' miners when he blew up the Gem mine over ta Coeur d'Alene. Governor Steunenberg is said to have a thousand dollars on his head. Man, we can't be associatin' ourselves with someone like that."

"That's Idaho," Larner dismissed with a wave of his hand. Then he sought to soothe the Scot. "Besides, you won't be involved, Angus. He'll be coming in under an assumed name and set up a local cover. I'll function as his sole contact with the Western Federation of Miners. Horsley is the only answer to a gunman like Steele. You know this Steele was one of Tom Horn's top triggermen, don't ye?"

"Bah! Horsley and his infernal machines." Angus glowered, then made his most telling argument. "He got the union miners ran out of Idaho with his bloody-handed ways an' he'll do the same fer us. You mark that, Abe."

"Speaking of running people out," Abe said changing the subject, "what area do we hit tonight?"

Angus pondered that a moment, still not satisfied with Larner's plans. "I'm thinkin' o' the west side. There's several families o' them furrin' dagoes set up with most o' the menfolks workin' the swing shift at the Holy Moses. We should be outta there before Steele and his damned gunnies know where we are."

The lobby of the Windsor Hotel, like most others in Denver, was a busy place at the stroke of six in the evening. On her second night in town, when Charity made her grand entrance via the sweeping stairway, a hush descended and heads turned. Within three strides she became the focal point of all attention. She flushed at the tangible wave of raw male lust and lowered her gaze. Not, however, before noticing a striking figure among the throng.

Over six feet but with a slight stoop from carrying two heavy crates the man in question radiated an aura of something beyond the ordinary. His merry blue eyes glittered with admiration and humor. Carbide gaslights flickered from sconces on the walls, giving him a ruddy, sun-browned glow. He winked to acknowledge her interest, then bent to place the crates on the floor in the center of the large oriental carpet.

Charity couldn't see what he did with them because of the mob milling about. Yet suddenly pandemonium erupted around him. Ladies screamed and fainted; there came a furious yapping of dogs, and men went into a hilarious knee-jerk run that seemed not to carry them anywhere. In the midst of this bedlam, the tall man stood erect once more, then pushed through the crowd toward Charity. In a flash, a flurry brown rat exploded from under the jigging feet, with a tiny, wirehaired terrier hot on its naked tail. Understanding came to Charity and she began to snicker.

"The moment I saw you on the stairs, I knew you would appreciate my little joke," the man began without preamble as he reached her side. He took her hand in his. "Right then I dedicated it to you." Charity found herself looking into those merry blue eyes from quite close up. "Allow me to introduce myself. I'm Capt. Lyulph Gilchrist Stanley, Lord Ogilvey, heir apparent to Airlie."

Icicles hung from Charity's words. "I'm Charity Rose of Dos Cabezas, Arizona Territory. My grandfather was a tenant of your grandfather, I believe."

"Ah, yes, our Irish estates. I certainly hope he managed to escape that unpleasant stew," Ogilvey replied, entirely unruffled. "Already I'm making efforts to dispose of our holdings there . . ."

"How, ah, noble of you," Charity grated.

She tried to maintain a stern and disapproving demeanor, only to dissolve into actual giggles when the frantic little terrier caught his prey, skidded on locked legs, and slammed into the back of a portly gentleman's knees. The rat escaped, the dog yelped in pain or fear as the chase resumed, and the red-faced victim made clumsy effort to regain his feet. A tall man in evening dress dug at a writhing lump under the back of his Prince Albert while a pair of frustrated terriers leaped at his legs, adding their shrill voices to the din.

"Do you do this sort of thing often, Mr. Ogilvey?" Charity gave up all pretense at severity and the question was asked in frank curiosity.

"Captain Stanley," Lord Ogilvey corrected her. "Actually, not exactly. Rather wanted to rupture some of the pomposity around here, d'you know?" Stanley smiled winningly. "Livened things up a bit, what?"

"Indeed you did. Oh-oh. Things are getting messy," Charity observed.

Captain Stanley looked around and saw that there were several dead rats, some of them lying in pools of blood on the carpet.

"Oh, dear! I rather doubt the dining room here will recover tonight, and I'm famished. Would you join me for dinner at the Brown Palace? Afterward we shall go to the Occidental. Stephanie, Baroness diGallotti, is doing *Tannhauser*. Should be a rather smashing evening, what?"

For a moment Charity considered a waspish reply, then allowed her instincts to overcome her prejudices. "I'd be delighted."

Bowing obsequiously, the waiter at the Brown Palace delivered two silver bowls of flaming brandied cherries. Despite her discomfort at being seated so long, Charity's eyes widened in childlike delight at this unfamiliar treat. Lyulph Stanley took it all in stride.

"Another glass of champagne?" he asked her.

"No, thank you. I'm getting quite light-headed as it is," she replied, green orbs sparkling with reflected blue flame. "Ah, how do you eat these? I'd think the flames would . . ."

Lord Ogilvey chuckled sympathetically. "It dies out, then you dig right in. There is a special treat to this. Under the cherries is a mound of *gelato,* what people in your country call ice cream. That's why the dish is called Cherries Jubilee."

"Fascinating . . . ummmmh! And delicious, too," Charity enthused.

Ogilvey drew a huge, thick, gold-cased watch and studied its face. "We'll make it just in time. Fortunately, the manager of the Occidental arranged a box for me."

"Ummmm. I could quite easily learn to live like this all the time," Charity responded. "Only I fear I would soon weigh two hundred pounds."

"Not with the, ah, proper sort of exercise," the young baronet said with a certain twinkle in his eye.

"Why, sir," Charity returned in mock alarm. "One might suspect were trifling with my affections."

Stanley's expression changed to a serious mask and a warmth radiated from his deep blue eyes. "I never trifle, dear Charity. When I set out after something, I'm quite serious."

A chill, chased by a thrill, ran down Charity's spine.

Seated three tables away, Dr. Marcus McDade and his companion of the evening dined in a somewhat detached manner. Young Dr. McDade had noticed the entrance of Lord Ogilvey and a stunningly beautiful young woman. He had no idea who she might be. He'd not encountered anyone so lovely, though he would certainly like to. He ate mechanically and the young woman in his company sensed the detachment. Likewise the cause. Inwardly she seethed.

Two boxes, to each side of the stage, could be reached by narrow passageways between the outer and inner walls of the second floor Occidental Hall. When Charity and Stanley entered theirs, heads turned and admiring glances blossomed for the handsome couple. Lord Ogilvey need not have worried about seating. Despite the sensation created throughout Denver by the arrival of Baron and Baroness diGallotti, the theater was only half full. When it was determined no latecomers remained to be seated, the stage manager gave a cue and the curtain rose.

Gasps came from the audience at the sight of the spectacular backdrop, which depicted a Rhine castle and a flock of crows in a scarred and blasted forest of gray trees. A grand piano sat alone at center stage. After a moment, to allow the audience to adjust, Baron Carlos diGallotti entered from stage right.

He was impeccably dressed in evening clothes. His complexion was sallow, his cheeks thin, with a bushy mustache that remained glossy black, despite the gray at his temples. He walked with an erect, military bearing. When Stephanie diGallotti entered from stage left, it became immediately obvious that her husband was a good half inch shorter than her five foot eight. Although thirty-two years of age, Baroness Stephanie looked closer to twenty. Her husband, slightly balding, clearly showed the thirty-five years difference in their ages. Baroness Stephanie sparkled when she walked.

Diamonds, sapphires, and emeralds glittered on her fingers, around her gloved wrists, at her neck, and in the puffed gores of her silk costume. She also affected a small tiara of large, blue-white diamonds. Her long, black hair had been done in a fashionable and fetching chignon. Dark brown eyes flashed to either side of her rather prominent nose, and her olive complexion had a ruddy glow of vivid health. She and Don Carlos made slight bows to the audience and the baron seated himself at the piano.

An abbreviated arrangement of the overture to *Tannhauser* vibrated from the strings of the piano. Few had ever so clearly mastered the complexity of Richard Wagner's blending of psychological and dramatic themes in the lyric form as Stephanie. Her rich contralto enthralled the small audience, although hardly a one could understand the German words. Charity came close to tears when Stephanie—playing Venus, who had been transformed by Wagner into the Nordic goddess Freia—sang the lament over Tannhauser's departure from the Court of Venus to recover his immortal soul. When the final curtain wrung down, a white-jacketed attendant appeared at the curtained entrance to the box.

"Lord Ogilvey, the Baron and Baroness diGallotti request you and your guest's presence backstage in their dressing room."

"Thank you, my good man," Stanley said affably, stuffing a gold eagle into the usher's hand. "Please inform them that we shall be delighted. And would you send someone out for champagne for us? The Brown Palace has an excellent American vintage, ah, Cook's it's called."

"Right away, sir."

"Gil." Ogilvey had persuaded Charity to use his preferred name. "Will we be able to stand up during this?"

"Why is that, my dear?"

"My, ah, my back is causing some discomfort," Charity invented, covering for the painful location of her recent wound. "I wrenched it recently and long spells of sitting tends to make me awfully sore."

"I'll see to it myself, Charity," Lord Ogilvey assured her.

Charity had never been backstage before. She'd not been in a theater more than twice in her life. The hustle and bustle of stagehands and the dim light gave it a romantic air. She could feel her emotions stirring as they approached the door to the dressing room.

"Oh, do come in," Stephanie effused when she answered the knock.

Introductions were quickly made and in minutes the champagne arrived. Gil Stanley deftly opened the bottle and poured four glasses. These he passed to their hosts and Charity, then lifted his in a toast.

"To the finest performance Denver has ever experienced."

"Why, thank you, Lord Ogilvey," Stephanie burbled. "I must admit to a tiny disappointment at the size of the audience. Anything less than a full house is so depressing, don't you know? Nevertheless, I have decided to abandon the rest of our concert tour and remain in Denver for a while. The dry, high altitude climate is just what dear Carlos needs for his lung trouble. Perhaps we can plan another performance here later on."

"Oh, I hope so," Charity enthused. "You sing so

beautifully," she added, repeating her earlier compliment.

"Thank you, my dear. Now, let us repair to the City House, where we have a light repast laid on."

Eat again? Charity asked herself. And to *sit down!* How could she possibly do it? Ah, the life of the rich and famous.

Chapter 6

Talons gripping a high pine bough, an owl hooted an indignant challenge to the two-legged creatures invading its domain. Another of its kind echoed the angry sentiments. Thirty grim-faced miners, keeping as quiet as non-woodsmen could in the forest, ghosted through the trees in the direction of the small Italian settlement outside Creede. Along with the usual pick handles, they carried sledgehammers, axes, *flambeaux* torches, and tins of kerosene.

"Keep it quiet," Angus McRoberts hissed, troubled by the crackling stomp of boots. "Them dagoes got sharp ears."

"Who says that?" Stumpy Gordon, a powder man from the Denver City mine inquired.

"Never mind. Just be quiet," Angus growled.

Despite the racket they created, the miners managed to burst in among the tar paper and pine shacks without being detected. When they kicked open the flimsy door to one, a woman's scream alerted the rest of the community.

"Grab her! You boys get them brats," Stumpy Gordon shouted.

"Drag 'em out, boys, drag 'em way clear," another miner directed as he splashed kerosene on the wooden frame.

"No!" the woman shouted. *"Per favore, signores,* notta my house."

Three black-haired children, not a one over ten, ran shrieking from the grasp of the invading miners. Wood splintered in another shantytown dwelling. The occupants protested fearfully in Italian. A lad of eleven or twelve stood defying those who would seize him, swinging a length of chain and cursing hotly in his native tongue.

"Sons of asses, and sons of sons of diseased whores, leave us alone. I spit in the dead eyes of your mother. A thousand imps of hell descend on your heads."

One clever miner stepped forward and feinted with his pick handle. The boy lashed out and his chain wrapped around the hickory shaft. Too late he realized his error. Before he could disengage, the miner yanked him forward. A hard-knuckled fist in the mouth lost his weapon and put the youngster down. But not out.

He bounded up from the damp, pine needle-strewn ground. Moonlight turned the blood trickling from his lips black and flashed silver-blue off the keen edge of the stiletto he grabbed up from a fallen Italian miner who worked for the strikebreakers. The needle tip jabbed and wove fearful magic in the night air. While two miners remained in front of him, Angus McRoberts maneuvered around behind. When the right moment came, McRoberts snagged the boy under his bare rib cage with one burly arm while with the other he reached out and plucked the dagger from the lad's right hand.

The little guy wriggled like a fish. One elbow caught a cheekbone and Angus's head set to ringing. The kid rammed his skull backward and loosened a tooth. Groaning, Angus let go and the lad scampered out of sight.

"There's more of them to take care of," Angus prompted. "Keep at it, boys."

Half a dozen of the unionists had beaten two strikebreaking Italian men into bloody mounds that lay motionless under the cold moonlight. Within twenty minutes every shack in the small community had been leveled or set afire. There didn't seem to be anything left to do. Angus summoned his night raiders.

"We've done good work this night, boys. Maybe now these dago tramps will know we mean business. It's all of us against the owners or we'll never get anywhere. The union, boys, the union," he brayed to the groaning, weeping and whimpering residents of the West End.

"You go back to the mine, every man-jack of ye," Al Larner added, "an' ye'll get worse than this."

A sensation of utter uselessness swept rapidly over Charity Rose. She sat in the Ladies Parlor of the Windsor Hotel. She had found it necessary to sneak a newspaper into the stuffy room of velvet plush furniture. Only airy pulp romances, a book of poems, and stacks of sheet music had space in the parlor. The weighty subjects of the world were not for fragile female minds to contemplate. Now she regretted obtaining it. The Leadville *Herald-Democrat,* like the *Denver Post,* was filled with stories about the mining strike. Now came the latest news of the vandalism and fires in the Italian shantytown at Creede. Charity knew she missed a prime opportunity to pick up some wanted men.

Such types regularly gravitated to the violence of strikes and other union-backed disorder. The problem was that Charity's lovely bottom had not completely healed and she had considerable pain and difficulty when she attempted to sit a saddle. In spite of her gloomy outlook, she had to admit her time had not been unpleasantly spent. Rather taken with Gil Ogilvey from the outset, Charity had continued to enjoy his company whenever possible. As a matter of fact, she bided time right then until he would arrive for an engagement they had that afternoon.

"Today we're going slumming," he had told her that morning when they met on the street. "Some of that mob that were along to Stephanie's reception the other night want to see the seamy side of town. So . . ."

"So you thought of me, is that it, Gil?" Charity teased.

"Oh not at all. Balderdash! I thought about who would make the most pleasant company for me.

And that, it turns out, is you."

To Charity's great relief, a fancy drag showed up fifteen minutes later. Lord Ogilvey drove a spanking six-up, and the interior was filled with laughing, slightly tipsy young people. Gil escorted her to the carriage with all the pomp of an appearance at court. With a crack of the whip and lusty shouts, they set off for "The Slaughterhouse," Murphy's Exchange, at 1617 Larimer Street.

When the gleeful group entered the notorious dive few of the patrons paid much attention. They had grown used, of late, to the swells paying afternoon visits. Few, they noted with a certain smugness, did after dark. Leading the way to the bar, Lord Ogilvey introduced Charity to Johnny Murphy, the proprietor. After the amenities and an order for a round of drinks, Gil nodded toward a small cluster of men near the far end of the bar.

"That's Cort Thompson, a hardcase from long back, and Mattie Silks's solid man. Next to him is Henry Gilmore, a top-drawer gambler. That fellow beside Gilmore is Cliff Sparks, Doc Bragg's ex-steerer. The gem he's wearing is a diamond stud, worth two thousand five hundred dollars. He calls it his "headlight."

"What about the nervous little man next to Sparks?" Charity asked, her professional interest perked up by the thumbnail biographies.

"Ummm. Bad sort, that. Bill Crooks. His name sort of says it all. He's a tinhorn, a cheat. A while back, in October I think, Troublesome Tom Cady used his sword cane to belabor Henry Gilmore, who has been calling himself Jim Jordan lately.

That was in the Missouri Club. There's bad blood between them, so the story goes."

Her sixth sense tingling right wildly, Charity studied Jordan-Gilmore and wondered if he might make the next contribution to her war chest. She started to inquire more about his background when two men entered. One was short, with a thick, black beard. The other stood over six feet and had the shoulders and arms of a logger.

"Oh-oh, I think we may have chosen an inopportune time. That's Soapy Smith, so-called King of the Thimbleriggers. With him is his shell man, the same Troublesome Tom Cady I mentioned."

No sooner had their eyes adjusted to the interior than Tom Cady made a menacing flourish with his sword cane. Not about to be battered again, Jordan whipped out his gun. In an instant, six-guns blazed. Bystanders scattered, screaming or cursing. Another shot sounded. Johnny Murphy and his bartender, Mark Watrous, poked their heads above the bar top. When the gunsmoke cleared, it revealed a bloody scene.

Cliff Sparks lay gasping his life out alongside the brass rail. Kneeling at his side, saloon owner Johnny Murphy lifted the wounded man's head. In keeping with their gambling origins, he made Sparks aware he was dying.

"Cliff, old man, they're off at Sheepshead, and you're last."

"I'm last," Cliff repeated faintly, then convulsed and died.

His pal, Tinhorn Bill Crooks, rushed forward and shoved Johnny Murphy aside. Dropping to his knees beside the body of the slain man, he cried out in anguish. "They've killed my dear old pal!" For effect he sobbed wretchedly. "They've killed my best friend, Cliff Sparks!"

He then clasped the dead man tight against him and, sobbing uncontrollably, pressed his face close to Cliff's blood-splattered breast. Removed somewhat from the drama, Charity Rose watched while Bill Crooks, as he wailed his fathomless grief, robbed his dead friend by biting the twenty-five hundred dollar diamond stud from the bosom of Cliff's soiled shirt. Making note of that, Charity determined to report the incident to the officers later. Tin pipe whistles shrilled and the nearest policemen came on the run.

"Tally-ho!" Gil Ogilvey piped up. "And I think it's time for us to make a strategic, if hasty, retreat."

Back under the tassel-edged roof of the drag, the young swells of Denver chattered excitedly about the slaying while Ogilvey whipped the bays into a run. Three policemen dashed inside Murphy's and the occupants of the drag could hear the clang of a Black Maria's bell as they rounded the corner. Rocking wildly, the coach careened along another block. At the last minute Gil Ogilvey decided to make another turn.

Disaster waited in the change of direction. As the coach rounded the block, it rode high on two wheels, then suddenly flipped onto its side. Young women shrieked in horror and men tumbled about in the rear of the rig. The wreck pulled painfully at Charity's stitches. She winced and bit her lip to keep from crying out. One of the bays made a continuous, almost human scream of pain, its right foreleg broken. More police whistles sounded.

Groaning, Charity extricated herself from the wreck and leaned against a street lamp pole to regain her equilibrium. A kindly, rotund policeman trotted up. Scampering behind him came a group of ragtag street boys. The peace officer immediately took in the situation and mercifully shot the injured animal.

"This is Doyle's rig," he said, speaking to the wide-eyed youngsters. "One of you boys run off, quick like, and inform him of the accident. Now, miss . . ." He turned and started to address Charity, only to observe a great deal of the back of her legs and her wriggling bottom as she delved into the carriage to pull out one of the frightened young women trapped there. "Bejazas!" the thoroughly male lawman breathed out reverently at sight of her well-turned calf.

With the officer's help, Charity pulled free the less fortunate of the passengers and began to staunch their bleeding. With clanging bell an ambulance arrived. Ignoring the pain in her buttock, Charity aided the ambulatory victims aboard. It seemed to Charity that only seconds had gone by since a freckle-faced lad sped off to inform the hostler, when that worthy arrived, red-visaged and seeking more than his fair share of recompense.

"That horse," he thundered, pointing at the dead, fifty dollar nag, "was worth three hundred to me. And the drag'll cost another two or three hundred to repair. I'm holding you, sir, responsible. Pay up or we'll take this matter to court."

"Here, here, old fellow. No reason to get upset," Lord Ogilvey began soothingly. "All in a day's excitement, what? Here, let me . . ." He trailed off as he produced his thick wallet and counted out a thousand dollars. "Surely this should heal your material and emotional loss, eh?"

Beaming, Seamus Doyle hastily pocketed the currency before the potty Britt came to his senses and demanded it back. Wasn't every day a son of Erin could put it over on a snotty English toff. Unaware of it, Charity shared Doyle's opinion, though for a different reason.

Charity was far from pleased with the English lord. Her anger surged upward in the place of fear and relief at being alive and unharmed. First, she took mental stock, he had taken them to a scurrilous dive, where they witnessed murder and robbery and could have been harmed themselves. Then that mad dash away to avoid confronting the police, which ended in such tragedy. He'd risked all their lives and caused a fine animal to die in agony. All for an afternoon's excitement. It wasn't that she remained particularly frightened, nor had she been during the gunfight. But she risked her life for a living and saw no humor in someone else recklessly calling the shots, and for no good reason. Hands on hips she confronted the lackadaisical lord.

"You have one fine nerve, my good fellow," she started, deliberately mocking his manner of speech. "What ever possessed you to take us into that frightful place with the prospect of a killing at any moment? And why did we leave hell-bent for leather? *We* were not suspect."

"I, ah, simply thought it a good idea at the time."

"You *thought?* You haven't had a reasonable thought this entire day. Damn you, sir, I don't like other people risking my life for me. I don't like them assuming they can lay out a whole lot of money and walk away blameless from a horrid accident. And most of all, I don't like you. Don't bother hiring a cab. I'll walk to the Windsor."

Chapter 7

Like a gaggle of geese, and even noisier, a score of barefoot urchins — boys ranging from eight to twelve — hurried along one of the rutted lanes called streets in Independence. The camp had sprung up around the Vindicator mine at Cripple Creek, Colorado. A few girls, in flour-sack dresses and cotton cloth aprons, and even some toddlers, joined the parade. In spite of the low clouds and threat of rain, the youngsters were off to see their hero, Harry Orchard.

Harry Orchard was a handsome, sandy-haired young miner, with charming mannerisms and a fondness for children and baseball. When he first came to Cripple Creek, he took a job as a mucker at the Vindicator, in defiance of the union miners. He soon had a tidy little cabin which, a number of local wives were wont to say, he kept "neat as a pin." Harry soon became noted for his devotion to

Abner Doubleday's great sport. No matter how long the shift, or how tired he might be, Harry could always be found after work in a poorly leveled, sand-covered lot, coaching, umpiring or participating in a game of baseball.

Most of the adults of Independence saw him as a neat, easy-going fellow who encouraged the children of the community to rummage in his jacket pockets, where they found a ready supply of candy and other sweets. Although now the mines had been closed for several weeks by the strikes, Harry never lacked for treats to dispense to the youngsters, many of whom hardly had food to eat at home. He didn't want for work, either. The previous week he had spent time collecting donations from saloon keepers and individuals to pay the parson's salary. When he turned in the contributions, the church committee noted that not so much as a dime was missing. He had also raked level the infield at the ball diamond. His honesty, generosity and happy-go-lucky demeanor caused much speculation among the naturally dour miners.

Some said he was a defrocked minister. Others suggested he was the scion of a wealthy eastern family, sent west to make a man of himself. Another faction spread the belief that Harry had struck it rich in a glory hole somewhere to the west of Cripple Creek and, from a saintly nature, doled out his wealth to his less fortunate brethren. None of them, save Abe Larner, had the slightest idea that *Harry Orchard* was the alias assumed by Albert E. Horsley, the notorious mad bomber of the Idaho gold fields.

Today was *the* day. The axe wound Charity Rose had received had finally healed. Not only did it signify that she could return to her profession, it also meant that today she would give the smugly disinterested Dr. Marcus McDade his comeuppance. To achieve these goals, Charity had chosen carefully. After a bath in a hip tub, a bonus offering of the Windsor Hotel, she had laid out her finery. The time had come to vest herself and go forth to the contest.

Lips compressed as though in deep concentration, eyes half closed and distant, she approached the bed with slow steps. Arms extended, she lifted the fancy black silk panties. Critically she observed them in the mirror attached to her commode and vanity table. Bending down, she stepped into the leg holes and slowly slid them up her long, gracefully curved legs. Taking her time, she turned to examine the fit and drape in the pier glass. Another leisurely stride to the bedside.

Charity reluctantly added a sturdy, front lace foundation garment. The whalebone stays would accentuate her trim figure and youthful bosom, yet its stricture displeased her. Next she lifted a gossamer chemise of palest green and elevated her arms so the garment fell over her head and torso in a verdant cascade. A clarion note sounded in her head: the summons to battle. Visions of how she would conduct the three parts of the combat occupied her consciousness. Now came a voluminous petticoat, split-legged and tiered in emerald flounces from waist to mid-calf. She could almost sense the nearness of her prey. Satisfied with the proper placement of each accessory, she came at last to the stunning green silk gown. Another clarion sounded as she checked the overall effect.

Her dark auburn hair hung in thick sausage curls, a part also in her plan. All she needed was her hat. Charity selected one with a broad brim, bold flare, cocky feather, and no veil. The final brassy summons echoed in her head. Armed with her parasol, Charity stepped into the arena—er, the hallway—and walked confidently to the head of the staircase. Glancing askance, she checked out the effect on the occupants of the lobby as she descended the stairs. Encouraged by the admiring glances of the males and envious glares of the ladies, she marched resolutely to the door and out onto the street.

Dr. Marcus McDade felt like he had been dragged a hundred yards by a galloping horse. He had been up all night, delivering not one, but three babies. Mrs. Calhoon had come to term at ten in the evening. Mrs. O'Banyon brought young Liam Marcus into the world at one-thirty. Just as he was about to take gratefully to his bed at two-fifteen, Bruno Hauptstetter rapped urgently on his door and dragged the doctor off to deliver his wife

Anna of a pink, squawling daughter. His eyes burned and the hell of it was he hadn't time to catch even a nap before he opened the door for office hours.

"Coffee," he suggested aloud to himself, not really expecting the bitter brew he usually concocted to be of much effect.

The bell over his outer door tinkled gratingly on his strained nerves. There followed a husky, though sweetly intoned voice. "Good morning, doctor."

Marcus McDade turned to see an achingly lovely vision of feminine pulchritude. A green goddess, he amended as he took in her startling attire. "Er, I don't believe I've seen you before," he stammered out.

"Oh, but you have," the beauty teased. "At the Brown Palace, the Windsor, around the town with Lord Ogilvey. Even at the opera house the other night."

"Y-you've come as a patient?" McDade queried.

"Yes. A bit of unfinished business, shall we say?" Charity tweaked him. "Our first encounter, if you recall, really left me in stitches."

"Why, I . . . I . . ." Thoroughly bemused, the good doctor could not place his patient.

"Oh, perhaps I erred. I was certain that memory of me would have dogged your path these past weeks," Charity coyly added.

"I—ummm, ah, that is . . ." McDade fumbled.

"I'm positive this is the appointed date and time for you to place gentle hands upon my derrier," the lovely young woman boldly stated.

"Well, I . . .that's an unusual way of . . ." Sudden realization dawned on Marcus McDade. This vision of glory and the manish female bounty hunter of the axe wound were one in the same! And she wanted—wanted . . .

Visions of her well-turned legs, silken rump, and narrow waist flooded the doctor's mind. His mouth went dry and he began to breathe like a steam engine. Thoroughly in heat, he tried to reconcile the images with the reality. It only made matter worse for him.

"My stitches, doctor. You were to remove them today," Charity came out plainly. "Perhaps if I assumed the position again, it might remind you." So saying, she hiked up her dress and bent over the desk. "If you'd be so kind as to slide down my petticoat, doctor?"

"I . . . ummm . . . gaaah . . ." Stricken inarticulate, Dr. McDade advanced on his patient and complied. His heart thudded and his hands quaked with the effort.

"Ah, that's much better. I'm afraid I have both hands quite full. The, ah, the undergarment, too," Charity instructed.

Marcus McDade silently cursed the fiery waves radiating from his loins and the protruding bulge of his engorged phallus. "P-perhaps y-y-you'd prefer to use the screen and a hospital gown?" he forced out.

"Oh, this is quite all right. You considered it good enough before, remember?"

"I had no idea. I mean . . . I . . ." he declared in a quavering voice.

"The panties, doctor?"

"Aaaah, er, yes. Right away."

He nearly tore them he shook so hard. Raw lust throbbed at his temples, and his fatigue retreated in the face of his ardent mood. Gathering his resources he began to remove the sheer black silk. Drops of perspiration popped out on his upper lip and his forehead became a lake, In an absent-minded manner, he searched for scissors and began to snip the bits of catgut. By now his hands shook so badly that he feared he might knick the silken flesh. An ache rose in his gut.

"If you'll, ah, turn a bit, please," Dr. McDade requested in a distant voice.

He set to work on the last few sutures, which followed the curve forward from her pert buttock. Charity noted his hands quaked so violently that he found it necessary to brace the back of the one holding the scissors against her pubic mound. Exercising astonishing muscular control, Charity flexed her womanhood spasmodically and hoped she had grown wet enough for him to notice. According to her plan, she made no effort to control the flinches when sutures came out. In fact, she accentuated the effect by wriggling in a pretty, seductive manner and voiced the sexiest little moans she could manage.

"Aaaaah! Oooooh, doctor." Charity added the finishing touches on her vocal effects as he bathed the area with alcohol after spending an inordinate time retrieving the bottle Watching his fumbling hand in a reflection from the glass door of a medicine cabinet, Charity suspected rightly that the doctor was too entranced watching her posterior to make an accurate search for the bottle. At last the time came for Dr. McDade to pull up her panties.

He did so reluctantly, taking an interminable time to put them in place. The petticoat came next. Charity could almost feel the effort of will this required. Marcus McDade sighed heavily. Charity kept her back turned as she adjusted her gown, though she sensed his presence lingering, uncertain. Arranging her expression to one of starstruck wonder, she wet parted lips and turned to face him.

"Miss Charity, I . . ." McDade squeaked like an adolescent.

The embrace was instantaneous and expected by both. Nevertheless Charity barely managed to turn her head in time to avoid his fevered lips as he sought to kiss her with erotic abandon. She pushed firmly against his chest and produced a cynical smile.

"I'm not your type, doctor. Remember?" Charity said harshly.

She felt him go rigid and leaned back to look into the handsome features, now red with fury. Coldly she laughed. For a moment she thought he would strike her. In a rush of honesty she conceded to herself that she deserved it. Marcus released her and stepped back. Anger ebbed to embarrassment for both of them, and Charity hurriedly left the office before she had to listen to the apology which Marcus ached to offer her.

Sunlight winked off the nickle-plated copper badge Sam Steele wore on the wear-softened front of his wool shirt. Seasonably warm that day, he had shed coat and vest and tied them off behind his saddle. The bay gelding he rode snorted with frisky anticipation of lush green grass and a soothing rubdown at the end of the trail. Steele had recently been appointed a deputy sheriff after increasing union violence had driven off the lawman he replaced.

"Hull damn thing don't figger," Steele said aloud to his horse. "So far the miners have done all their own dirty work. Worse, the mine owners don't want to hire pr'fessional strikebreakers. No sense in that a-tall. Them Eye-talians and Chinee are willin' enough to work, but the first little roughin' around an' they disappear like smoke. I tell ya, horse, we're in for some rough times one way or another. There ain't enough of us to corral all the miners, and there ain't enough of them to face down our guns. Sooner or later, the union organizers are gonna get wise to that and bring in some bad-ass like that bastid Horsley, an' the world's gonna get turned upside down."

Steele heard a sharp crack and felt a ripping tug along his side. The next instant, white-hot pain exploded in his chest. He heard the heavy boom of what he judged to be an express rifle a fleeting moment before pain-numbed shock blacked him out.

Hanging like a great bronze disk in a brassy late afternoon sky, the sun still baked the prairies of eastern Colorado. Panting in the shade of a sumac bush, a kit fox bitch watched warily as a coyote sorted out the confused trail she'd left. Her dugs ached for the litter she'd whelped, yet she wouldn't return to the burrow with death for a shadow.

A nervous glance at that deadly presence told her that she would soon have to make another run for it. Tensing, judging carefully which way to spring, the kit fox discerned in the distance the squeak and rumble that warned of the coming of the big, two-legged creatures. Assailed it seemed by enemies on all sides, she crouched low and suppressed a whimper of desperation.

Ears not so keen as those of the kit fox, the questing coyote continued his search for several minutes. then the man-sounds registered sharply and his instinct for self-preservation sent the dog-like scavenger loping away across the tall grass plain. The source of the disturbance grew nearer, watched anxiously by the small, black, beady eyes of the kit fox.

"By dang, I say it's a waste of time," a grizzled old-timer mouthed from a tangle of bushy, graying beard. "They're gonna get tried by a *state* circuit court judge, ain't they?"

"Uh, sure they are, Zeke," the younger man on the prison wagon agreed.

"Well then, what diff'rence it make if they get tried in Denver or sent back like this to the county where the crime was committed? I say it's just more work for us and a dratted expense to boot. Somebody's got to pay our wages, pay the judge, the hangman, all that."

"The state does that, Zeke," the youth responded.

"You ain't lookin' at that right, son. You listen a spell to me, Billy. Government ain't got no money of its own. They get money by takin' it from the people in the way of taxes. So it costs us, you an' me, a powerful lot more to haul prisoners to the county seat where they done their crime and hang 'em there. I don't take to the government strippin' my pockets to put on a fancy show in Las Animas. This bunch could swing jest as good in Denver as there, for all I care."

Thoughtfully, Billy posed a theory. "Maybe it has to do with the justice side of it. Maybe the folks in Las Animas, or Raton, or Creede want to see the ones done them wrong punished right before their eyes."

"Revenge, is it, Bill? Wall, it don't bother an iota if these folks have their vengeance firsthand or not. Keep it simple and cheap, I say. Lord knows there's enough people to hang it could bankrupt the state to get them all."

"We're gonna want to camp soon, huh?" Billy asked, to change the subject. "We want to be set up a good while before dark."

"Yep. That's as usual. But I got me this favorite spot by a crick that's well worth the waitin' for. I mind how it weren't safe to make camp near water when I first came out here. If a buffalo or elk herd didn't tromple a feller, like as not a band of wandering Injuns would pay a call. Wasn't for a lot of years before anyone, even the Injuns, would camp close to runnin' water. 'Course these days the buffalo are 'most gone and folks have moved the bucks and squaws onto the reservations. Might as well take advantage of the less dubious aspects of civilization, I say. We kin get a bath an' stop stinkin' like skunks, and enjoy lettin' the crick burblin' over rocks lull us to sleep."

The voice faded before the high-pitched squeal of a dry axle. When that, too, dwindled to silence, the relieved kit fox bitch made haste, bounding across the ground on stubby legs. When the wagon reached the chosen spot, the sun had already set. Billy dismounted and opened the padlocked rear door to the prison wagon.

"All right, step out easy now," he commanded, covering the prisoners with a shotgun. "You can go relieve yourselves and get freshed up at the creek."

Being young, inexperienced, and a humane fellow by upbringing, Billy unlocked and removed the long chain that connected them. Shotgun held ready, Billy escorted the pair to the creek.

"C'mon, youngin'," the other prisoner whined. "How can I wipe my ass with my hands cuffed in front of me like this?"

"You gotta go, huh, Gimpy? Well then . . ." Billy said through a soft chuckle. He undid the cuffs and produced some convenience paper from inside his hat brim. "Squat over there."

Unexpected and chilling in its raw power, a scream of agony came from farther up the creek. Then three rapid shots followed. The sequence carried signature all its own, unmistakable and undeniable. Torn by indecision for a moment, Billy dithered over his dilemma.

"Ain't nowhere you two can go in leg irons. Just stay put till I find out what's happened."

So saying he rushed off to help his friend. Zeke lay on a large rock at the water's edge. He had been bitten on the left hand by a baby rattler. Billy found him and rushed to administer what aid he could.

"Dang fool doin's if there ever was one. Go an' pull a tenderfoot stunt like that," Zeke complained between groans of pain. He started to rise to a better position and Billy gently pushed him back.

"You just sit there. I've got to make a tourniquet and try to get the poison out." The young guard set to work at once.

Using his trousers belt and pistol barrel, Billy fashioned a tourniquet and applied it to Zeke's upper left arm. With his sheath knife he cut X marks on the puncture holes and began to suck out the poison. The bitter orange, numbing fluid and blood he extracted he spat to one side, intent on his rescue mission. Zeke continued to complain throughout the procedure. When Billy finished, he began to fashion a bandage.

"I'll have to loosen that for a bit to prevent mortification," Billy said as he applied the dressing.

In mid-sentence Norbert Klinger spilled over the creek bank with a single tree in one hand, which he had removed from the wagon. His legs still shackled he landed clumsily, though within striking distance. Before Billy could react, Klinger brained him with the solid oak billet. Blood already running from his ears, Billy sank to the ground, and fell across Zeke. With a wild cackle, Klinger leaped across both men and began to strangle the driver with his chains.

"He-he, can't keep ol' Bert down, no sir, that they can't," he muttered over and over while the driver's struggles lessened. "Oh, no, can't do no harm to ol' Bert."

When both victims proved satisfactorily dead, Klinger searched for the keys on Billy's corpse and shed his chains. Like a caricature of a prehistoric hunter, he dragged the bodies back into camp and built a fire, all the while cackling about how no one could put a rope to ol' Bert. After a while, his eyes registered on the other prisoner, a kid being returned on cattle rustling charges, who sat cowed against a wagon wheel. Rising, he limped swiftly to the boy's side.

"By dang, I plumb forgot about you, boy. The

Lord he works in mysterious ways, don't he? We're free now," he added as he opened the lock on the lad's leg irons.

"No, please. I don't want to be let loose."

"Why not?" Klinger roared. "The Lord has provided and we must be grateful for His goodness."

"Please, mister. I didn't do no rustlin' and I can save myself in court. I don't want no murder charge tacked on my tail."

" *'Murder'* " Norbert Klinger howled. "It weren't murder. The Lord delivered us out of the hands of the Philistines. You're sinning against the Lord's will to stay in them chains." Anger rising, eyes glinting with a crafty notion beyond his quasi-religious rambling, Klinger saw a new reality. Straightening, he glowered down at the youth.

"If you ain't fer ol' Bert, then you're again' ol' Bert. The world's filled with sinners an' it's my mission to punish them." So saying, he bent and refastened the shackles, securing the boy to the wagon wheel.

Quickly, for his odd, gimpy walk, Klinger went to the corpses and used a butcher knife to remove their heads. With the ungainly hobble of a cripple, he returned to the wagon. Holding the heads by the hair, their mouths agape, he used them for cudgels as he pounded the terrified boy senseless. When he satisfied himself that the youngster had expired, he dropped the heads beside the limp form and moved to the fire.

Humming a scrap of a gospel song, Klinger prepared a meal. He ate it with gusto and rolled in fresh blankets for the night. Oblivion soon claimed Norbert Klinger and only then did the young prisoner dare to open his eyes. He stared in horror at the battered heads set to either side of him, then looked beyond to the sleeping form of the madman. He would have to play possum until Klinger rode away in the morning. That he knew for certain.

"Gonna fool ol' Bert. Gonna fool ol' Bert all night long." The pitiful thought kept repeating in his mind as he spent a sleepless night.

Chapter 8

Itchy, stiff, and generally uncomfortable in their Sunday best, Cyrus Bennett and his family sat down to their Sabbath dinner. Maybell Bennett had instructed the cook to take particular care with the plump goose which she, as lady of the house, had gone to considerable expense to secure for the feast. The occasion was more than a celebration of the Lord's day. This was little Jimmy Bennett's ninth birthday. There would be a cake afterward, and hand-cranked ice cream. Jimmy, in honor of his achievement of nine years without a fatal disease or mortal accident, would get to lick the dasher all by himself. His father, as a prominent member of the Cripple Creek Mine Owners Association, believed in simply stated ostentation, a phrase he had coined several years before.

Right then Cyrus Bennett would have preferred a little less ostentation and one of those hand-cranked ceiling fans to move the thick, midday air. They had a servant boy, Joshua, the cook's boy, who could operate it for a few pennies. With all the family gathered at last around the table, including three of Jimmy's closest friends, Cyrus cleared his throat loudly. Heads bowed and hands clasped at this signal for devotions. In a rich baritone, Cyrus intoned the seemingly endless prayer.

Quickly growing weary of it, Jimmy and his companions suppressed giggles while they pinched each other on bare legs above knee socks. Seven-year-old Sarah heard the rustling and opened one eye. Seeing what was going on, she whispered loudly in Jimmy's ear.

"I'm gonna tell."

"You do an' I'll pull the head off your dollie," Jimmy retorted.

At last the senior Bennett wound down to a conclusion. "Bless us, O Lord, and for that which we are about to receive, let us be truly grateful."

What Jimmy Bennett received was a large, wet blob of his father's brains. Glass tinkled and everyone present heard a sharp, meaty smack a moment before the sniper's heavy bullet from an express rifle exploded Cyrus Bennett's head into chunks that adorned his family, the walls and ceiling, and the snowy linen tablecloth.

Left side throbbing, Sam Steele sat across the desk from Sheriff Drummond. The chief lawman wore a worried expression and his eyes darted from object to object, refusing to fix on the angry deputy confronting him.

"I say it is the only way. Weren't no three-dollars-a-day miner who could afford that express rifle that popped me," Steele stressed. "The damn union's started importing professionals. Now's the time to get rid of them."

"But I don't know, Sam, about this running them out," Drummond protested weakly.

"We round up the leaders and the key members, give 'em one-way tickets out of Colorado and put 'em on the train. What's so difficult about that?"

"The, ah, part about what happens if they come back," Drummond offered.

"It's self-preservation, sheriff. Either we get tough now or we get swamped later."

Sam's side pulsed with fiery waves of pain that spread through his body. His head ached and he still wondered why his assassin had not finished the job. Whatever the case, he was alive and he intended to do something about this new threat from the miners' union.

"I—I suppose I'll have to go along. Make sure, if you will, Sam, that it's the guilty parties."

"If I could be sure of getting the guilty parties, I'd have 'em in jail right now."

"Whatever," Drummond dismissed with a wave of his hand. "Do your best."

"You can be sure of that," Sam Steele promised darkly.

"Face it, you were a beast," Charity Rose said to her mirror.

Restless, and feeling guilty over the way she tormented Dr. Marcus McDade, Charity left her room for another dinner alone. The urges of her healthy young body made strident demands, which the image of the handsome doctor only exacerbated. In an attempt to banish this persistent temptation, she had recently begun to daydream about her first love, Corey Willis.

Only thirteen at the time, the two friends had turned a challenge: to go skinny-dipping together—into a wildly erotic afternoon. Charity had joyfully surrendered her maidenhood to towheaded Corey's inept, but sincere, efforts. She could almost feel again the magic of their first coupling. The thudding of her heart and roughness of her inhalations rudely brought Charity back to the entrance of the Windsor Hotel dining room. She entered and seated herself at a table in one corner. The waiter took her order, looking at her rather oddly. Charity wondered if her eyes sparkled like they did on the long-ago summer day.

When her meal arrived, she found it flat and tasteless. Glancing around the crowded dining room, Charity found several men who were aware of her, yet none who really appealed. Eager for distraction, she considered visiting Baroness Stephanie, whom she sincerely liked, but rejected the idea. She didn't want to run into the Ogilvey crowd. Despairing of any enjoyment from her food, Charity left her meal half eaten and took her leave. As though rejecting the world, she hurried to the exile of her room.

In her absence, Charity noted at once, a bellboy had been there. On her dressing table lay a cone of tissue paper, filled with a dozen long-stemmed roses. A white rectangle protruded from their midst and she opened it with nervous fingers.

"My dear patient," it read. "Please accept these roses as a peace offering. And please accept my invitation to dine with me tonight. I shall call for you at nine o'clock." It was signed, "Marcus."

Suddenly the world became a bright and interesting place again. Charity began to hum a lively Irish ditty as she prepared for bed. The roses had been a wonderful touch. Though she could hardly go running at him at an invitation. She'd let him stew a while, say until *tomorrow* evening. Then she could "accidentally" encounter him on the street, thank him for the roses and perhaps consider a reconciliation. Nude before the mirror, Charity ran her hands over her body.

Instantly her caress brought to mind the doctor's touch over her derrier. In a flash she was covered with goose bumps and slipped her green silk nighty over her head. Heart pounding again, she jumped in bed and pulled up the covers. Visions of white-haired Corey and curly blond Marcus interchanged behind her eyes. Wide-eyed, they stared at her. Oddly enough, they shared the same body. A reasonable image, she decided, since she had only seen Corey, not the doctor, unclothed. For a wild moment, Charity wondered what the doctor would look like, standing naked before her as Corey had so often done. Would his manhood excite her as greatly as Corey's had? Hell yes, she decided with a shiver, only more so. There was a knock at the door.

Jolted out of her erotic fantasy, Charity timidly inquired as to whom it might be. "Dr. McDade," came the answer.

She'd forgotten he had said he would call for her at nine! "G-go away. I—I'm indisposed," she answered uncertainly.

"I'll not go away. I have to talk to you. Even if you won't go to dinner, I must see you."

"No, you can't. I, ah, mean . . . it's hardly fitting, is it?" Charity hastily evaded.

"I am your doctor, after all. Besides, if someone reports me standing outside your door with a bucket of champagne, the management might evict you," McDade answered cheerfully.

Glancing down, Charity saw her swollen nipples. Fragments of her steamy imaginings whisked through her consciousness. With a smooth surge of effort, she came out of bed and started for a wrap. With the frilly, tenuous covering clinging to her shoulders, she hurried to the door and opened it.

"Come in quickly," she began without greeting or preamble. "The noise you've made I'll be surprised if they don't throw me out."

"Gladly, sweet vision," McDade responded, taking a swift stride across the threshold.

Forgetting again the appointed dinner hour, yet

acutely aware of her erect nipples, Charity continued in a snappish manner. "What's so damned important at this time of night?"

"Why, my invitation to dinner," the doctor said lightly. "Though it's obvious you're not prepared for that. In truth," he said, growing more serious, "my conscience forced me to apologize for my boorish behavior when first we met. I can't bear to let the night pass without your forgiveness."

"The—the roses were lovely. Smell them." She sniffed deeply. "They fill the whole room with their scent."

"As do you, dear . . . Charity," McDade returned. His expression was that of a heartbroken little boy.

Touched and aroused, Charity found the words of forgiveness spilling from her lips before she'd given conscious consideration to them. In return for her kind dispensation, Marcus McDade took her in his arms and tenderly kissed her. For a moment she did not respond. Then her own burning desire fanned flames into her lips and they writhed against his. She gasped when he released her.

His voice roughened, Marcus spoke with averted eyes. "I'll, ah, open the champagne."

He did so and poured two glasses he had conveniently brought along and handed one to Charity. "To us," he toasted. "And to our joyful relationship."

"What relationship is this?"

Marcus set aside his wineglass and collected hers

as well. Then he embraced her again. His kisses were hot and lingering against her smooth forehead, eyelids, nose, cheeks, lips, and neck. With each fiery touch, flashes of her kissing experiments with Corey illuminated Charity's brain. She responded with an ardor repressed for over a month. Her tongue probed its way into his mouth, seeking mysteries. She moaned softly when he pressed against her, and she felt the bulk of his straining erection. Marcus sought out one firm, round breast and fondled it lovingly.

Charity's hand slid from the back of his head to his neck, then down and around until she clasped the rigid length of his manhood. Marcus began to tremble. His fingers, stiff as a neophyte's, fumbled at her dressing gown. With an eagerness born of flaming desire he pulled it away. Charity, oblivious to propriety, worked frantically to undo the buttons of his shirt. Marcus shrugged out of his coat to make it easier for her.

"My nightdress," she panted in his ear. "Let me get out of it."

Marcus released her and pulled off his shirt as she bent to the hem of her filmy green sleeping gown. With practiced ease she divested herself of her last bit of clothing and stood radiantly naked before him. His wide-eyed stare rewarded her with a thrill. Her hands flew to his belt, unbuckled it, and undid buttons at his fly.

"Oh, God, hurry," Marcus moaned, fearful he would reach completion before they had consummated their desire.

A spike of sheer delirium pervaded Charity's body as she welcomed Marcus's fullness within her. She wound her legs around his waist, and her body pulsed with each magnificent thrust. Waterfalls and star bursts erupted for both of them as they blended and tested experience. Mutual endurance paid benefits for loved and lover alike. When at last the universe swallowed them it happened as a single outburst of translucent splendor.

"I always knew Corey was great," Charity said dreamily, "but never like this."

"Who is Corey?" Marcus asked, lying beside her.

In the times between delicious bouts of splendidly erotic lovemaking, Charity told Marcus all about her first true love. Rather than deterring his flaming passion, it seemed to feed it the more. Pale dawn showed pastel pink and white on the horizon before they lapsed peacefully into deep sleep.

A cracked, off-key bell rang jubilantly in the small clapboard church in Cripple Creek, which also served as a schoolhouse. A sea of well-wishers flocked around outside, and invited guests filled the narrow interior of the dual-purpose building. Standing before the altar were Reverend Parkhurst, the widow Baker, and Harry Orchard.

"Do you, Harry, take this woman, Mildred, to be your lawful wedded wife? To love, honor and cherish her, for richer or poorer, in sickness and health for so long as you both shall live?"

"I do," Harry croaked.

"And do you, Mildred, take this man, Harry, to be your lawful wedded husband? To love, honor and obey, through sickness and health, for richer and poorer, until death you do part?"

"I do," Mildred cooed, eyes sparkling with unconcealed love.

"Then, by the power vested in me by the Almighty God, and the authority of the State of Colorado, I now pronounce you man and wife. You may kiss the bride, Harry."

Blissful, the couple embraced. A tired, battered, wheezing pump organ groaningly began the Mendelssohn wedding recessional and the crowd spilled out behind the happy pair. Rice flew and flowers as well. Several men fired off their six-guns and the children ran shrieking. Mildred's three youngsters, boys twelve and eight and a girl nine, swelled with pride when they heard the remarks of a couple of neighborhood gossips.

"I'm simply delighted, Hattie. Harry is considered quite a catch among the single ladies of town. Mildred is so lucky."

"Yes, she is, Gladys. He's so good with children, too. I hear Jamie, Charlotte, and Brian adore him."

"That's what Mildred told me. And he thinks the world of them. Made Jamie a regular home-run hitter, whatever that means."

"And he's gone back to work at the mine. Working while others foment trouble."

"You're right, Hattie. Such an industrious man. A regular breadwinner," Gladys concluded.

At the flower-decorated carriage, the newlyweds paused. "Are you sure it will be all right, Harry?" Mildred asked anxiously.

Harry gave her a beaming smile and a peck on the cheek. "Of course I am, my love. Jamie's quite the young man now. I know he'll take good care of his sister and little brother while we're gone. After all, it'll only be for four days."

Harry handed her into the rig and vaulted up beside her. Taking the reins, he snapped the rumps of the sprightly team and they sped away for a blissful, if short, honeymoon.

"All right, come on out of there," Sam Steele growled. "Hidin' under the bed will do you no good."

Grumbling, another striking miner crawled into view. Steele and two deputies frog marched him out the front door and added the hapless fellow to some twenty-seven already collected. Since six in the morning they had been rounding up all the union members, herding them down to the railroad station, where other lawmen kept them under detention in a stock corral.

"Whatter ye doin' to us, ye blitherin' idiot," the cranky miner asked testily.

"You're all gettin' one-way tickets out of Colorado," Steele announced for the first time. "Your families will have time to pack up and follow once you've located somewhere else. If any of you troublemakers return to Colorado, you'll be shot on sight."

"That's again' the Constitution," one grizzled powder man declared.

"The Constitution be hanged. Yer troublemaking days are over. No more bombs, fires, or beatings of loyal men who want to earn a day's pay," a mine manager, along for the show, informed them.

"Move along now," Steele commanded.

Only one day back from their honeymoon, Harry and Mildred Orchard witnessed the roundup from their front porch. The suddenly developed plight of the wives and children tugged at Mildred's heart.

"Oh, it's so heartless, Harry. Isn't there another way?"

"Aye, Mildred, it's an outrageous shame. Yet, what else can the poor, embattled mine owners do? They can't tolerate the violence these unionists spawn, even though there are men like myself to put in the longer shifts. And they can't give in, even if there were not men willing to defy the union. Just trust in God that justice will out. I'll be leaving here soon, too," Harry added, changing the subject.

"How's that, Harry?"

"I have to make a little trip to Denver over next weekend," Harry replied.

"Oh, that's a shame it is. I'm sorry you must travel around so much, what with your long hours in the mine and the volunteer work you do for the church and all."

"It's a burden easily borne, my dear," Harry told Mildred. "Trust me."

Chapter 9

Blackest night hung over Denver, Colorado. The moon had set early and the stars were masked by a thin, high scud of clouds. A mournful bawl from a cow in the stockyards awakened Charity Rose. She stretched languorously and yawned. Then, still sleepily, she rolled over to nuzzle Marcus McDade's cheek.

Her lips moved with growing awareness and fervor as she progressed to his ear, down his neck and between his bare shoulder blades. Rapidly she became excited, remembering the fantastic lovemaking they had generated during the long hours before midnight.

Marcus had barely awakened when a sound from outside froze Charity.

There, it came again. From the balcony. Someone was cautiously trying the door that opened onto the widow's walk. How had he gotten there? Abandoning her pleasure, Charity leaped from bed and darted to the bureau.

"What is it, Char? What's wrong?" Marc McDade asked groggily.

Charity dug a Bisley Colt out of the top drawer and glanced at the face of the cylinder to assure herself it had not been inadvertently unloaded. Still naked, the raw passion barely subsided within her, she turned toward the narrow, curtained door.

"Charity, what is it?" Marcus demanded louder.

"Sssshush," she quieted.

She crossed only another three feet when she heard footsteps retreating with an oddly irregular cadence. Klinger! She had heard he had escaped from the prison wagon. In a rush she reached the door, threw the bolt and swung it open. A part of the same motion, she fired the Bisley at a dark bulk that rounded the corner of the building.

Klinger spun and flame erupted from the muzzle of the six-gun he had taken from young Billy, the prison wagon guard. Splinters flew from the planking near Charity's bare toes and another slug screamed off the brick wall beside her head. Her target momentarily shielded by the corner, she dived back inside. Quickly she noted that her lover had sprung out of bed and now made a flurry of wild activity. Realizing her own nakedness, Charity threw a shot around the doorframe and dived for her dressing gown. A glint of street-lamp light on honed steel called to her attention that Klinger had left his axe behind. At once she started across the room.

Thoroughly rattled, Dr. Marcus McDade pulled on his pants while Charity selected a lucifer match from a small dish and prepared to ignite the gas jet. "Don't show a light, Char," the doctor shouted to her. He began to stamp into his fancy boots, muttering while he did. "By God, the scandals would be bad enough to ruin my practice as it is, let alone getting shot in a lady's bedroom. Who is that madman?"

"Norbert Klinger. Remember, he escaped from the sheriff's custody in the jail wagon?"

"Well, I don't care who he is. I've got to get out of here," Marcus went on as he jammed his pearl-gray Stetson on his head.

Five rushing strides put him out onto the balcony. Excited voices and running footsteps sounded from the hallway beyond the door. From the widow's walk came another bellow from Klinger's .45 and Marcus scrambled back into the room on a beeline for the hall door. Thoroughly disgusted at her love's antics, Charity started to take another shot at Klinger.

"Don't shoot again," Marcus commanded in a stage whisper. "No one's out there."

Hesitantly, Charity eased her way onto the balcony, then cautiously approached the corner of the hotel building. She remained close to the rail, yet careful not to brush it. Seconds dragged as she got into position. She took a deep breath, then did a fast shuffle to where she commanded the stairway and next length of the walk. No Klinger.

Light from a street lamp glinted off a roughly circular surface. Charity bent low and discovered a small pool of blood. She stiffened at the sound of hurried footsteps behind her and made ready to swing around with the Bisley ready. Heart pounding, she waited until the last second, then turned rapidly.

She came face-to-face with Dr. Marcus McDade. Avoiding her eyes, he brushed past and down the stairs. Too disgusted to hurt, Charity sighed heavily.

"At least his reputation is intact," she said dejectedly.

Head down, Charity returned to her room to find the door broken in. The hotel manager, in trousers and nightshirt top, the house detective, bell captain, night desk clerk, and several hotel guests she could not identify milled about. When they caught sight of her, everyone began asking questions at once.

Charity rapidly lost patience. Fortunately the beat cop poked his head in the room a moment later.

"Flarity," Charity called to him over the constant uproar. "I didn't ask these people in my room. Would you please clear them out?"

"Right away, Miss Charity," he answered obligingly. His Irish tenor voice turned to a bellow. "All right now! Everyone out! G'wan, all o' ye, except Mr. Dennis an' Mr. Gower," he added, naming the manager and house detective.

With order restored, Charity gave a thorough report of what went on, omitting only the presence of Dr. Marcus McDade. Damn the man, she thought vehemently. Yet she kept him out of it, her body still warm from the pleasure they had shared. When she finished, the house dick gave her a fish-eyed stare.

"I frankly find that a bit hard to believe, miss," he pronounced in round, rolling syllables. "Word is that you've been entertaining a gentleman up here, in violation of the rules. Could it be you two had a falling out tonight?"

"Why, I . . ." Charity began, fury blazing from her eyes.

"That's enough o' yer dirty-minded talk, Paddy Gower," the beat cop snarled. "Happens I'm acquainted with the case in question. Miss Charity here indeed did apprehend Norbert Klinger. When the extradition came through from Kansas, he was packed off in the prison wagon to be tried and hanged. He escaped on the way. Killed old Ben and Billy and left another prisoner a babbling madman."

"I'm terribly distressed that you underwent such an ordeal," Raymond Dennis, the manager, burbled, wringing his hands. "All of this has caused you considerable inconvenience and I must apologize. The best the hotel has to offer is not too much for you. We would be happy to change rooms for you also. And we'll keep the location off the register and a secret, if you like."

"You're very kind, Mr. Dennis. For the time being, though, I would be content if you arranged for a maid to pack what things I leave here and put them in storage. I'll be leaving shortly after sunup on an extended business trip."

Abner Waterford joined the ranks of early risers the next morning. He attended a prebreakfast meeting of the Mine Owners Association, then repaired to the Brown Palace for a substantial meal. He was headed for his carriage in front of the Brown Palace Hotel as Charity, in her guise of C. M. Rose, rode by in a cab and headed for the livery stable. She looked out at the millionaire speculator and gave him a friendly wave. At the same time she saw a man walk past the rear of Waterford's buggy. Any name escaped her, yet she thought he was vaguely familiar. She still pondered this when Abner Waterford shouted.

"Look out! That's a bomb!"

A bright flash and powerful concussion followed an instant after Waterford dragged his driver to safety. Smoke and dust filled the street. Horses screamed in mortal agony. In a twinkling, Charity saw again the pleasant, handsome face and realized whom it belonged to. Albert E. Horsley, Coeur d'Alene's mad bomber. In a blur of motion, Charity bailed out of the cab with the carpetbag, which contained her weapons, in an attempt to give chase.

Too much off balance, she had to stop and put the Lawrence rig around her slender waist. As she did, she cursed her luck at having left Butch behind, in the care of young Sammy Pierce, the Windsor bellboy. By that time, Horsley had disappeared. Quick looks along a side street and up an alley yielded nothing of use. A passing teamster on a beer wagon reined in at the sight of the carnage.

"Did you see a man run from here? Which way did he go?" Charity demanded of him.

"Nope. I done saw him before that blast, but I didn't see what happened after. Too busy fightin' my team. Comes to mind I've seen him before, up Creede way, I reckon."

Stymied, Charity returned to check out the site of the explosion. Already, she noted, the vultures of the press had descended. Three of them simultaneously asked loud, abrasive questions. With the skill of one accustomed to the press, Abner Waterford answered them in turn.

"What caused you to be suspicious, Mr. Waterford?"

"Well, being an old hard-rock man, myself, I recognized the smell of burning fuse and then saw a wisp of smoke from under the carriage. From there, my body just took over and did what it had to."

"Then you saved the coachman and the young

lady? How'd it happen you managed to grab them out of the way?"

Abner pondered a moment. "Don't rightly know. Seemed the right thing to do at the time."

"I was riding by in a cab when the bomb went off," Charity injected. "When I saw you move, I couldn't help but admire your courage and fast thinking, Mr. Waterford," she concluded, noting the little blonde who shivered in terror on his arm.

She also saw the faint lines of healed scratches on the girl's face. Abner, thinking her a man, first showed affable pride at the compliment, then, observing her direction of interest, displayed all the symptoms of insane jealousy. Whistles tooting, the police, and a bell-clanging ambulance, arrived. Charity recognized Patrolman Newman and took him aside for a moment.

"Ed, I wasn't thirty feet away," she began, then told him what she saw, leaving the teamster's information out.

By then, Abner had begun to suspect her gender and grew increasingly hostile. "By the way, young man, why didn't you use those cannons you have around your waist?"

Eyes taking on a brittle jade cast, Charity stared him down. "I didn't have them out, or on at the time. If I hadn't had to stop to strap them on, I would have at least winged your bomber."

"You needn't listen to his abuse, Miss Charity," Ed Newman offered solicitously.

That did it for Abner Waterford. His face

twisted into a mask of revulsion and contempt. "Talk. That's all you can expect from a pants-wearing, gun-toting bitch. Come along, my dear."

Ignoring those around him, Abner retreated to his suite. Charity, her feelings hurt by the ungrateful millionaire, proceeded to the stable, retrieved Lucifer, and walked him to the Denver Union Station. The blaring noise of a mechanical band, playing the last few bars of "Maggie Murphy," reached her ears. The tune ended and immediately began again. She purchased her ticket and made arrangements to put Lucifer on the stock car.

All the while, the automated, two octave pipe organ-snare drum-cymbal-trumpet played "Maggie Murphy" over and over. "It's sort of like my life lately," Charity observed of the jammed instrument as she guided Lucifer into the loading chute. Finally, with her faithful companion loaded, she found a seat in the day coach.

"Off for the scenic ride to Creede," she commented sarcastically to the matronly woman across the aisle.

It's day all day in the daytime,
and there is no night in Creede.

C. M. Rose's arrival proved Cy Warman's oft-quoted ditty. The camp pulsed with riotous activity while she unloaded Lucifer at three the next morning. The "scenic" ride had included a large rockslide where rain-softened earth gave way and tons of boulders had fallen onto the track. A crew of gandy dancers already labored at the site when the Daylight Special slowed to a stop.

For the next five hours, robins, finches, cardinals, and mountain warblers put on a colorful show and entertained with trilling music. Many of the passengers, including C. M. Rose, took it in stride, creating a picnic atmosphere by spreading blankets, breaking out hampers of fried chicken, sandwiches, cold beef ribs, and other delicacies. At last the main line had been cleared and the Special proceeded. More than a few train patrons had to be awakened when at last the chuffing Baldwin locomotive pulled into the Creede Station. Now honky-tonk music blared in competition with the new and obnoxious ragtime from a dozen stews along the main street. Off-shift miners surged in and out of the gambling halls, their movement influenced by raucous-voiced barkers and the quantity of liquor they had consumed. Unlike her entrance to Denver, the gun-hung, black-garbed stranger attracted little attention.

Although tired, Charity decided to look over the lay of the land before retiring. After seeing to her animals, she gave priority to Soapy Smith's Creede operation, the Orleans Club. She knew Soapy to be back in residence after his Denver sojourn and running his soap scam with Doc Baggs. As she walked through the streets toward his establishment, Charity recalled what she knew of the notorious con man.

Jefferson Randolph Smith was born in Georgia in 1860. By the time he reached Denver, he had devised a variation of the shell game that employed cubes of soap, a cheap and plentiful commodity. Dark-eyed, slender, a dapper, genteel, and thoroughly glib Soapy Smith soon earned the nickname as "King of the Thimbleriggers." Vigorous, and in his twenties, the bearded Soapy enlarged his operation by taking on Doc Baggs.

Baggs was listed in the 1882 city directory of Denver as a "Traveling agent." He was, in fact, a big-time con artist. He always wore a glossy stovepipe hat and carried a silk umbrella. Already in his declining years, Doc had somehow been convinced to join forces with young Soapy Smith. He was the first of Soapy's gang Charity spotted when she entered the Orleans Club.

Doc stood at the back of a crowd gathered around a layout at the far end of the bar. From the midst of the crowd a lyrical voice chanted hypnotically.

"Use this soap and wash your sins away! The Good Book says that cleanliness is next to godliness, but the feel of good, crisp greenbacks in the pocket is paradise itself. Step up, friends and neighbors, watch me closely. What I'm about to do will amaze and confound you.

"First off, I want to offer to each of you gentlemen salvation in the form of one of these miraculous cubes of soap. All for just twenty-five cents, one quarter of a dollar. A bargain at any price. Step up. Who'll be first?"

Charity moved closer and saw the pile of soap cubes, a scatter of currency, and a stack of blue papers on the layout. Behind it stood the diminutive form of Soapy Smith. The marks looked from one to another, doubtful and restive. Some had played before. Some had scored a dollar or two; most took home nary a dime. From the midst of the crowd a querulous voice sounded.

"Oh, hell, Soapy, you know we can go to the gen'ral mercantile and buy *five* bars of soap for a quarter."

"Ah, yes, but not this special Miracle Salvation Soap, made with the Blood of the Lamb." Soapy paused and frowned. "Tell you what I'll do. You see before you this hundred dollar bill. If you want to take a chance on winning one of these little green papers with the big numbers on them, I'll sell you a wrapped bar for the silly little price of five dollars."

So saying, Soapy twisted the hundred dollar bill and, before the eyes of his rapt audience, apparently wrapped it and a cube of soap in a square of blue paper, which he tossed carelessly alongside the unwrapped pile. Swiftly his nimble fingers wrapped more cubes. In some he appeared to place one, five, ten, and twenty dollar bills. A few he took pains to show contained nothing. When the pile had grown, and along with it the avarice of the crowd, Doc Baggs signaled one of Soapy's cappers who hadn't been in the game for some time.

He stepped forward and gravely handed Soapy a five dollar bill. After careful consideration he selected a wrapped cake of soap and opened it. Shouting gleefully, he displayed a hundred dollar bill which he had found inside. Eagerly the suckers swarmed to take advantage of this astonishing get-rich-quick scheme. Charity, as C. M. Rose, held her place and watched. After a while, with disappointed groans and curses growing more numerous, Doc Baggs stepped forward and paid his five. Miracle of miracles, another hundred dollar bill. The marks flocked to the shearing.

One found a dollar, another a ten. Seven men in a row found nothing. Confident that she understood the skinning operation, Charity crossed to the bar. In a matter of moments, she had identified several wanted small-fry. Their presence didn't tempt her to blow her cover by arresting them, or to throw away her money on the fixed games. Her sharp eyes and quick mind had soon discovered that Soapy palmed most of the money. Only a little sucker bait and the big payoffs to the shills remained in the stack. The roulette wheel had a brake on it, one so clumsily applied it amazed her no one else suspected. Three Card Monte was only a variation of the shell game Soapy played with his cubes of soap. Gradually her thoughts returned to the petty criminals.

Many had prices of a hundred or so on their heads. There ought to be a way to cash in on them before they went big time and really hurt people. She had the advantage of appearing as either a lovely woman, or a competent bounty hunter. Surely she could use this to advantage and perhaps even snare some big name wanted men in the offing. Opting for a night's sleep, Charity left the Orleans Club.

She checked into the Columbia Hotel and wearily carried her gear up to the room. She had no sooner entered and closed the door, the lock not even set, than a knock came on the flimsy panel.

"Who is it?" Charity inquired in her husky voice.

"Timberline," came a sultry, feminine reply.

Charity opened up to reveal her caller, a freelance hooker. She stood in the doorway, hip-shot, a tall, angular young woman. Her looks, on a smaller female, would have been sheer beauty. At six foot two, she seemed a bit too much of everything. She produced a whore's smile.

"Howdy, li'l feller. You looked kind of lonely when you came in. Thought you might like a little company."

"I, ah—er . . ." Charity began.

What a fix, she thought in confusion. Dare she turn down the offer? Paper-thin walls and curious neighbors created a problem. She didn't want the town's underworld circles to know that she was a woman. An outright refusal could result in two unacceptable interpretations. The truth would finish her effectiveness. And she'd constantly be the target of town bullies if the word went around that C. M. Rose was a sissy. How would a man handle the situation?

"Th' name's Rose, lover, just like yours, only folks call me Timberline for, ah, obvious reasons. Won't cost you but five dollars, four if it's gold. We can have us a real good time."

"Really, I . . ." Charity blurted, feeling like a fool.

Timberline took the little hombre's indecision the wrong way. "Got yourself such a case of the hots you can't speak? You ain't payin' for conversation, lover. We're gonna make the bed squawk. Nothing like a little rumpty-dumpty, eh?" So saying, she gave the little guy a push to the chest that accomplished two things simultaneously.

It informed the huge hooker that she wasn't dealing with a man, but a woman. Likewise that, when a small fist smacked solidly against the side of her jaw and she abruptly and involuntarily sat down, her size had intimidated no one. Shaking her head ruefully, Timberline picked herself up off the floor.

"Ain't nothin' wrong, Jake," she hollered into the hallway to inform the clerk not to worry over the commotion. "Gee, honey, I'm sure sorry. I thought sure's hell you was a—"

Charity's hand over her mouth cut off the

bellow. After a moment, the auburn-haired fury removed her fingers. "Was a man. I ain't one for doin' it *that way,* so I guess this ain't a business call," Timberline went on in a stentorian explosion.

All the while, Charity tried to signal the big prostitute to shut up. She yanked her fully inside and slammed the door so the booming voice wouldn't carry all over the hotel.

"Will you *be quiet!*" Charity snapped furiously. "I'm dressed as a man and registered as C. M. Rose for a purpose. Your big mouth could ruin everything for me."

"Gosh, honey, I surely am sorry about that. I didn' mean any harm."

"I'll tell you the whole thing if you'll swear not to reveal a word to anyone," Charity offered the titanic tart.

"I'll do anything you say, honey. Believe me. I'll be happy to cooperate because I don't want the story spread that I made a play for another woman. People are all ready to believe the worst of a woman my size. They don't know how good a real man feels to me." Timberline finished with a slight sniff and wiped a tear from the corner of her left eye.

Now that she had an ally, Charity explained her reason for being there and the disguise as a man. She also showed Timberline the dodger on Albert E. Horsley.

"I'm positive I saw him in Denver yesterday. I'm also fairly sure he might be hiding out here in Creede."

Timberline worked her whole mouth, like a cow with its cud. "I think I recognize the likeness, but I can't quite place a name to the face. The only thing I'm sure of is that he's never been a customer. I'm new to Creede."

"When did you come here?" Charity asked, off on a new tack.

"Only two weeks ago. I'm my own boss, me'n Klugger. Outside of one quarter I split with Jake, the room clerk, I keep my earnings."

Charity questioned her closely, learning that Timberline came to Creede via Cripple Creek and that she frequented the Ford Exchange before setting out to work the hotels of an evening. Hookers saw and heard a lot, Charity knew from her association with the wagon train tarts in Kansas. Timberline might prove a valuable partner if Charity played her cards right.

Chapter 10

Perspiration ran in streams down the corded muscles of Charity Rose's neck. The fat man sat in a chair beside the bed and laughed wildly while he masturbated. Charity thrashed her head from side to side. She accepted money from another man who wanted to dress in a woman's clothing and pretend he was getting screwed by her. When her "trick" finally disappeared, she found herself straining atop the age-withered shanks of Abner Waterford.

"Enough of this," she heard her john demand. "I want you to get on all fours and let my friend here take you."

"No," Charity cried out in desperation. "Please, not that."

"You do it or I'll call the madam."

"Not her, oh, anything but not her. She hurts me awful. I—I'll do it if you pay me extra."

"Gladly. I'm a millionaire you know. Here."

Money changed hands. "Go on, pal, she's all yours."

In horror Charity saw the customer's friend to be Norbert Klinger, complete with bloody axe. Desperately she tried to tell Waterford that Klinger was a madman and that he would kill them both. Laughing, Waterford wouldn't listen and dissolved into Marcus McDade, who desperately crawled from beneath her and speedily donned his clothes. "I'm late, I'm late. Must think of my reputation, you know," he called squeakily as he ran for the window.

Klinger reached the bed and grabbed Charity by the waist. Something was going terribly wrong, Charity realized in dizzy confusion. She'd been paid to take both men at the same time, and now McDade was welshing and Klinger would have his way and kill her and . . .

Charity woke up at the crucial instant. A piercing scream still vibrated her lips and cold sweat soaked her nightgown. She ran a nervous tongue around her mouth and began to gag.

"Oh, God. Oh, my God," she said shakily. Never in her life had she so desperately felt the need of a good, stiff drink.

Nighttime was no bar to the Citizen's Alliance in Cripple Creek. Although without the input from Albert Waterford, they continued to function. This gathering had not been at their instigation. Sam Steele summoned them and served as the principal, and uninvited, speaker.

"I feel it is important to make each of you aware that by shipping out most of the union organizers and union member miners, banning them from the state, I have made it safe to hire the unemployed silver miners to work the Cripple Creek gold mines. I have performed this task at no little risk to myself and my men. The unemployed miners will turn in a ten hour shift for three dollars a day and the result will be a quieter town. The reason is that they'll be too tired for a lot of after-work partying."

"Frankly, Mr. Steele," Cynthia Gleason said as she rose to object, "we feel that you have been entirely too harsh in your methods. On several occasions you have been guilty of cold-bloodedly shooting down men for no good reason."

Steele produced a wry smile and a soft chuckle. With his left hand he pushed back the brim of the battered Stetson he had rudely refused to remove when he entered the room. "Guilt? Lady, I ain't felt guilt about anything in my life."

Cynthia was dumbstruck. "Now, see here, Mr. Steele, I . . . Gentlemen . . ." She appealed to the Alliance members around the table. "Gentlemen, are you going to let this—this *gunslinger* talk to a lady like that?"

"Now Cynthia, I think . . ." the mayor whined.

She didn't listen to the rest. By their shifty eyes, uncomfortable squirming, and gestures to silence her, it became apparent to Cynthia Gleason that Sam Steele had the men at the meeting terrified to oppose him. Quick to realize his advantage, Steele treated the lady with cold disdain, which eventually soaked in. Shrewd businesswoman she might be, but in the realm of diplomacy she was a fool. Cynthia proved it when she blurted out the thought foremost in her mind.

"You see what you've done, you whining curs? Now the town is hostage to a filthy gunfighter."

"No madam," Steele hastened to inform her. "Let me set straight a slight oversight on your part. My jurisdiction covers the entire mining district. Nothing happens, no one does or says anything without my approval. That includes you, madam. Even the sheriff has consented to my will. Do I make myself reasonably clear?"

Eyes still blazing defiance, Cynthia Gleason shivered in the imagined Arctic wind that encapsulated her and stared blankly at the plain of Armageddon that yawned open before her in her mind.

Hattie Conover performed a useful service, of sorts, in the community of Cripple Creek. By day she worked as a seamstress for the local millinery and ladies' shop. She was a young woman of modest means, who lived alone. She had a ramshackle cottage on the edge of Poverty Gulch that had a bare front yard and two window boxes which grew scraggly daisies and petunias. It was here that the twenty-year-old spinster conducted her nocturnal enterprise, which consisted of introducing the more adventurous of the community's youth to the joyful rites of Venus.

For the reasonable sum of one dollar, boys in

their teens could avail themselves of that which had so far been only the substance of imagination. The lad she entertained this evening turned out to be exceptionally young, and considerably nervous.

Jeremy Slade had always been considered precocious by his family and teachers. From the age of six, his vocabulary and solemn understanding of adult subjects had marked him from his peers. That this had not been a passing whim or subtle mockery on Jeremy's part proved out when he consistently chummed with older boys. No one suspected that he might be physically precocious until Jeremy was caught in the stable behind the Slade mercantile by his father, doing what in the vernacular was called "choking his chicken."

Companions of Jeremy, and notably, his father, resolved to put Jeremy on the "straight and narrow," self-abuse being considered by many as leading to one becoming a sissy. At last two teenage friends introduced Jeremy Slade to Hattie Conover.

Needless to say, the occasion, and his companions' graphic descriptions of what and how to do *it,* left Jeremy all thumbs. He quaked so violently he could not even undo the top button of his shirt.

"Here, Jerry, dear, let me help you," Hattie cooed soothingly.

Soon Jeremy was clothed only in a pair of cut-off summer longjohns. Despite his trepidations, he discovered he had a throbbing, urgently insistent erection. Hattie, by this time, wore only a thin, transparent shift. She trembled with delight as she stroked his silken, pale skin. Gently she teased him to even greater excitement. Jeremy began to wonder if he could "hold out" until the big moment. One small, feminine hand slid below his naval and delved beneath his longjohns.

Jeremy reacted as if given an electric shock. He gasped and his shoe-button black eyes widened as experienced fingers encircled his stiffened member. Hattie ruffled his curly ebon locks and brought forth a brave grin from the wildly stimulated boy when she began to stroke him. Swiftly then she peeled him out of his last garment.

"My, you're a real big boy," she said in praise of his endowments.

"I—I, er, get a lot of exercise," Jeremy said.

"I bet you do," Hattie responded thoughtfully as she increased the speed of her hand on his flesh. "That's probably why your friends sent you here."

Astonishment washed over Jeremy's face. "How'd you know?"

"Hattie knows everything. Now relax and let me get out of this and we can—"

Bursting open, the door cut off the rest of Hattie's remark. "Harlot! Seducer of the innocent! Beast of Baal!"

Norbert Klinger stood in the doorway, trusty axe raised in preparation for its grisly work. Shocked to immobility, the young prostitute and the boy faced him with horrified expressions. In two clumping, uneven steps, Klinger crossed the distance between them. The axe fairly whistled through the air.

Finely honed, the edge smoothly bit through skin, muscle, cartilage, and bone. Hattie's head leaped from a severed neck. Before Klinger could recover from his follow-through, Jeremy squeezed between the crazed killer's legs and ran shrieking into the night, stark naked. Behind him, Klinger cursed his missed opportunity to punish the sinning child, then set about arranging the scene as he wanted it to be found.

Stepping past the grotesque corpse, he jammed her head on the bedpost. From inside his canvas coat he produced a woman's wig of dark auburn curls and placed it on the gory trophy. "You're next," he chanted in a childlike singsong. "You're next."

He reset an overturned chair and neatly laid out the pair's clothing. Humming a few bars of "Let the Lower Lights be Burning," he studied his artful design, then slipped out into darkness.

In her guise as C. M. Rose, Charity settled down to a leisurely breakfast at one-thirty the next afternoon. Her tardy appearance earned a dirty look from the middle-aged proprietress of the Creede restaurant. A sniff of disdain accompanied the cup of coffee she brought, expressing her opinion of those who ordered breakfast so late. Her perfunctory attitude made it plain she didn't hold with young fellows who caroused all night and didn't get up until after noon. Still bothered by her nightmare, Charity paid her little attention.

She hardly noticed what she ate, either. With the last bite of biscuit, Charity decided to check out the Ford Exchange. The block and a half walk in the thin, clear air of the mountains whisked away all but a few lurking cobwebs of uneasiness. She entered the saloon and took note of the half dozen idlers lounging about. Turning to her left, she approached the bar and selected a place at the far end. She recognized Bob Ford behind the bar and ordered a beer.

While she nursed the brew, Charity considered her options for earning a reasonable sum by corraling the bountied men in Creede. The largest difficulty still revolved around how long she could keep the identity of C. M. Rose separated from Charity Rose. Ford worked her way, dusting bottles, and Charity noticed that he frequently touched a handsome neck scarf which he wore with some ostentation. Set four-square in the center of the paisley silk was a large stone. When the barman-proprietor drew nearer she offered conversation by mentioning it.

"That's a nice rock you're wearing," her husky voice declared.

"Oh, this?" Bob Ford responded, long, supple fingers touching the stone. "It's an opal." He removed it and placed the stickpin in her hand.

"It seems to have a life all its own," Charity observed.

Ford laughed lightly. "Yes. When you wear it next to your skin it glows even more. It's supposed to take the life force from its wearer. I suppose that's one reason people say that opals are bad luck," Bob informed her as he took it back and replaced it in his scarf.

"Hey, Bob, I done struck it rich!" a bewhiskered

prospector bellowed from the open doorway. "Why don't you fix me one of them fancy Sazerack cocktails, what ol' Bob Stockton whips up in Denver."

Bob Ford winced meaningfully in Charity's direction, then set to fill the order. Like the majority of his customers, Ford believed that whiskey was meant to be taken straight, without even the adulterating effect of branch water or ice. He placed the sugar, cognac, and aromatic bitters into the shaker, along with a few shards of ice, and placed a bitters-soaked sugar cube in the stemmed glass that would receive the concoction. He then covered and began to shake the metal container. He completed only half a dozen strokes when Charity observed his face go slack with terror.

"Ed," Bob Ford blurted out.

A fist-sized hole appeared in his chest and his body slammed into the back bar. The flat *blam* of a shotgun sounded almost on top of the impact of the load, and glass tinkled musically as bottles broke. Head ringing, Charity found herself sitting on the brass footrail with both Bisleys cocked and level on a tough-looking fellow with an eight-gauge Parker.

Both barrels issued wisps of smoke and a nine inch hunk of bar was missing from above her head. The startled shotgunner blinked at the brace of deadly .45 muzzles and licked his lips.

"Sorry to disturb you, friend. My quarrel was with that dirty, back-shootin' coward, Bob Ford. I'm Edward Kelly. I'm married to a sister of Cole and Bud Younger. I'm gonna put down this shotgun now, if you don't mind."

"What did you shoot him for?" Charity managed to gulp out.

"Why, he's the dirty little coward what shot Jesse James," Kelly responded as though everyone should know his purpose. "You moved so fast I just plain panicked and blasted at the blur. I didn't want no one else hurt, don't you see?"

Recovering herself, Charity came to her feet, the six-guns still pointed at Kelly. "You're willing to give yourself up, then? You'll come along with me without any fuss?"

"Yes sir, I'll do that. The deed's been done which needed doing and I'm content," he recited as though intending the words for posterity.

Charity scooped up the shotgun and, with Kelly in the lead, prodded him off to the local calaboose. The jail turned out to be a fifteen-foot-deep dry well, where the local volunteer marshal informed Charity that Kelly would stay until the next train to Denver. Having seen Charity's Graham County deputy's badge from Dos Cabezas, the marshal made her an offer.

"Mighty glad you was on hand, Mr. Rose. The town would be glad to pay you mileage and train fare to escort the prisoner to Denver for trial. I got to tend to things here an' there really ain't anyone else."

"Well, I'll consider it. With no wanted flyers on Kelly, it's the only way I can make anything on the deal. I'll let you know, marshal, before the day's over."

Charity had other considerations besides her pursuit of business, the shooting at Ford's Exchange, and the prospect of escorting the prisoner to Denver. This was recalled to her when Timberline approached her in the Dry Gulch Exchange.

"I just remembered where I saw that feller Horsley," the towering tart declared in her stentorian bellow. A frown from Charity lowered the volume. "He was gettin' off the train from Denver at Cripple Creek. It was while I was boarding for the trip here."

"Sooo," Charity drew out. "He'll probably have some sort of acceptable cover, or he would have been found out long ago."

Charity's mind clouded up and developed a brainstorm. She, too, would need a cover if she had to spend a long time searching out the high-priced outlaw. There were several that came to mind. What she needed was a reliable and constant source of information on happenings in the mining camps. Somewhere in the process, the idea of helping out Timberline mixed in with the rest. Then she had it. Charged with the excitement of it, she laid out her plan.

"Timberline, I've got an idea. I have a little money set aside. With it we could go into business. But not here in Creede. All of the good things are sewed up. I was thinking, perhaps, Denver, or Cripple Creek."

Eyes large in surprise, Timberline reacted with eagerness. "Oh, do you mean it? Really? Uh, what sort of business?"

"Well, what is it you do best?" Charity asked teasingly.

To the bounty hunter's surprise, Timberline took a moment to think that over. "You, ah, don't mean, ah . . ."

"Exactly what I mean. Only in this case you would be the madam," Charity assured her.

"Glory! Why, I've never dreamed I could—that is, it always seemed beyond my means. Say, I know lots of girls who would like to get into a really good house. They're not makin' anything on the streets here. Wouldn't take long to round them up."

"Then it's done? Good. Why don't you start gathering these girls, sound them out and get them ready. Don't take any unless they can cut it in a really classy operation. Here's money for train fare. I'll meet you in Cripple Creek in three days."

With her outlaw-catching enterprise under way, Charity hurried back to the marshal's office. To her relief she found the escort job still open. The afternoon train would depart in less than an hour, so the marshal hustled out the prisoner and turned him over to her. A metal band ran around his waist, with a padlock on the front and a loop behind. Through the ring ran a chain which attached his right handcuff to his left leg iron, and another fixed to the opposite extremities. It greatly inhibited movement. Charity nodded to Kelly and conducted him to the train station.

On the way, Kelly mulled over his situation.

Mistaking her Arizona accent for southern, he offered a proposition when they reached the waiting room. "I give y'all my word of honor that I won't try to escape. I'm willin' to shake on it."

Charity didn't understand the purpose or the need for a formal acknowledgement, but decided to go along. "I'll take you up on that, Kelly. It'll make the trip a lot less difficult for both of us."

Charity extended her hand and Kelly took it in his. His grip was an odd one, with little fingers twined, separate from the other; his index and middle finger extended along her wrist, spread apart. He even gave a particular sort of squeeze. Charity thought little of it at the time. Kelly, in turn, frowned slightly when he didn't receive the expected response. Once on board, they sat together in a red plush seat while the train rolled slowly out of the depot and on toward Cripple Creek and Denver. When the locomotive got up to speed, conversation lagged. After a while, Kelly made an unusual statement.

"Y'know, I won't do much time over this."

"Why's that, Kelly?" Charity inquired, not actually interested.

"Wal, it was a kill sanctioned by the Knights of the Golden Circle," Kelly smugly stated.

Charity frowned. "Who or what are the Knights of the Golden Circle?"

"Thought you already knew. Seein' as you don't have any idea of the wheeled cross, I got nothin' more to say."

And he said nothing all the way to Denver. Charity brought her prisoner to the central police station and had him booked. Try as she might, she could not find any wants on an Edward O. Kelly in the Denver collection of flyers. Tired, she went to the Windsor Hotel to spend the night. She planned to go on Cripple Creek in the morning.

Chapter 11

Sunlight glared on the fresh paint of the large sign:

Penrose & Tutt
Real Estate Agency

Dressed in her finest, Charity stopped a moment to admire the new broadside that proudly declared the largest land dealer in Cripple Creek. She entered and smiled winningly to a dude in eastern riding habit. He was tall, good-looking and soft spoken.

"How do you do, madam? I am Spencer Penrose. You may call me Spec. What is it you wish to do? Perhaps you are recently bereaved and wish to sell your late husband's property? I can guarantee the highest price."

"No-no, it's nothing like that. I came to buy," Charity corrected him.

His demeanor changed remarkably. Penrose affected a wolfish smile and waved expansively to include all of outdoors Cripple Creek. "Leave it to Penrose and Tutt to find you the very finest property at the absolute lowest price. Now what had you in mind? An estate? A business property? Mining claims?"

"Well, sort of . . . business," Charity hesitated.

"Ummm. A millinery shop, perhaps?" Spec offered.

"No. I had in mind a large, attractive building, something suitable to house a number of boarders as well as the business, or—ah, social quarters."

"I, ah, think I gather your interest. Would a large, old mansion be suitable?"

A trill of laughter answered him. "Mister, ah, Spec, everyone knows there are no *old* buildings in Cripple Creek. If you mean *run-down,* I don't have a lot of time to spend in fixing up. To be blunt, I wish to establish a large, and lavish bordello."

"Uh—huh!" Spence blurted, taken aback by her candor. "Might I suggest we have lunch, first, then survey the possibilities at hand in our listings?"

"Sounds delightful," Charity charmed him.

"Chad!" Spec called through the open-topped dutch door to a barefoot urchin sitting beside it. "Go to the livery and secure my white arabian, Rabbit. Be sure he's hitched to a trap and ready when I get there."

"Yes sir, Mr. Penrose," the moppet chirped shrilly. He thundered off in puffs of dust that his tough foot soles raised from the street.

"I'm terribly sorry to inform you that there is no decent place to dine in Cripple Creek before six in the evening. We will have to content ourselves with second best. The Auberge Bouchard is hardly Antoines, but they turn out fairly good New Orleans style meals. I hope you have a taste for *les cuisine creole*."

After the meal, Penrose escorted Charity to the livery, where the urchin, Chad, waited with a beautifully groomed arabian and a spanking black shay with red pinstripe trim. Penrose tipped the boy a quarter and helped Charity aboard. With a snap of the reins, they started off for a tour of available properties.

All along the Tenderloin, Spec Penrose kept up a flowing chatter about this or that building, its accommodations, location and potential. Rarely, and then only if asked, did he mention price. To each offering, no matter how glowing the account, Charity signified her disinterest. Half an hour passed and Spec presented the last one. Charity shook her head no before he began to extoll its qualities. A short time later, Spec reined in and looked slantways at his client.

"With one exception, I'm afraid I've exhausted all the suitable property in the Tenderloin, Miss Charity."

"Oh, I'm so disappointed. You've been so

kind, yet I swear I find nothing at all suitable."

Charity's disavowal didn't surprise Spec. He had been showing her the places indicated in order to establish what she did not want. Now that he had the client where he wanted her, he fired the first shot in a new line of attack.

"I'm not certain if you are acquainted with the late Pearl De Vere," Spec started out.

"No, I can't say I am," Charity prevaricated. The realtor's spiel had gotten to the interesting part, and she wanted to compare his claims with her knowledge.

Pearl De Vere, an assumed name, Charity felt certain, was said to have come from a good family in the East. This well-to-do family believed that she was a high-class dressmaker—the designer of De Vere Gowns for the wives of Cripple Creeks' millionaires. Actually she was the madam of the camp's most gaudy and elaborate sporting house, the Old Homestead on Myers Avenue. To this basic, and general, knowledge, Spec added only a few new items.

"So far as anyone knew, although the madam of a sporting establishment, Pearl had no known lovers. I say had, because she died one night last week during a lavish ball she threw. Some say to celebrate her death. Her funeral is this afternoon. Pearl was not the owner of the Old Homestead. It is, however, now up for sale. It's a three story, brick structure, longer than it is wide. It's quite a respectable-appearing building, except for the fancy curtains at the windows.

There are two indoor bathrooms to accommodate the, er, inmates and guests. Nearly every room his its own style, and there are a dozen heating stoves in all. There are crystal chandeliers in the parlor and lounge. The banquet hall has wallpaper of hand-painted traceries of laurel. It was especially ordered for Pearl from Europe. There's a carriage house, servants quarters above, a good well, a double-sided, three-holer outhouse, chicken coop, and a root cellar. It's situated on the center of three lots."

"It sounds ideal. What was the cause of Pearl's death?" she inquired, thinking of the lurking Klinger.

"An overdose of opium. She took her own life. No one has any idea why. However, the elaborate bash she put on in honor of her demise left a heavy deficit on the place. The owner feels compelled to sell in order to recoup."

"Who is the owner?" Charity asked, fascinated by the tale and certain it would be the right place.

"I'm sorry to say I have been sworn to secrecy on that matter. But I can take the commuter train to Denver this afternoon and have an answer for you by evening."

"That sounds wonderful. Yes, I'd like to know all about it," Charity enthused.

"Fine, then. In the meantime, you might as well take in Pearl's funeral. I understand it will be a major affair."

On her way to the funeral, to be held at Farley Brothers and Lampman undertaking parlor, Charity caught a glance of the latest edition of the Cripple Creek *Times*. An editorial adorned the front page, edged in black, with a headline reading, "Cripple Creek Can Bury Its Own Dead!" From it, Charity learned that the town in general had become indignant at the fact that Pearl De Vere's sister had disowned her upon learning of her true profession. That indignation had backfired on the family, and all Cripple Creek rallied around the deceased madam. With the newspaper clutched in one hand, Charity entered the mortuary.

Reverend Jim Franklin conducted the services, leading in several hymns, a Bible reading, then preached a sermon called "Let Him Who Is without Sin Cast the First Stone." A throng had turned out, mostly children and miners. Charity left the funeral early in order to observe the final rites. When the lovely casket was brought from the funeral home the procession formed up. The Elks Band led, conducted by their famous Joe Moore. They played a slow and solemn rendition of the "Death March." Next came the heavily draped hearse, with the lavender casket nearly hidden by a blanket of red and white roses. Immediately behind, a man walked solemnly beside the empty rig which Pearl had so fancied. The shiny red wheels and glossy black lacquer body glowed in the sunlight. It was pulled by a span of restive black horses. A large cross of shell-pink carnations lay on the seat. Four mounted policemen rode down the avenue, pushing back the crowd to make way.

Behind came a gathering of lodge members in brilliant regalia, trying to keep in step. The sight of their red fezzes, feathered helmets, and gold-braided scabbards sent thrills of ecstasy through the women in the crowd. Bringing up the rear, Charity saw buggies filled with thickly veiled women: Pearl's friends from the Tenderloin. By the time the procession reached the cemetery the sun had slanted toward Pisgah Mountain.

Charity had accompanied the mourners and stood to one side as they gathered around the open grave. Several among those attending said a few quiet words, then some of the congregation began to troop to their buggies. Four husky miners lowered the flower-covered casket into the ground, and the air shivered to the sad, sweet notes of Joe Moore's cornet as he played "Good-bye, Little Girl, Good-bye." Profoundly affected by this touching tribute to a lady of easy virtue, Charity turned quickly aside to wipe away tears that formed involuntarily in her eyes.

Dusk descended quickly on Cripple Creek. Spec returned, looked up Charity at the hotel and informed her he had good news.

"Let me take you to dinner at the Old Homestead and you can gain a better impression of all that is available."

"Isn't it closed, what with Pearl just buried today?" Charity asked.

"Oh, no. It never closed a day. The owner wouldn't go for that. Too much loss of revenue. The place really has the finest food in town."

"All right. I'd like to get a look inside. We'll go then," Charity informed him.

Plush burgundy drapes, lace curtains, and a jungle of potted plants adorned the interior of the Old Homestead, in addition to the fabled wallpaper and crystal chandeliers. The huge dining table was of rosewood, with matching, upholstered chairs. Glowing sterling silver service twinkled on the white linen tablecloths, and each place setting displayed the finest Easton bone china. Each piece of furniture, including the baby grand piano, was of the finest quality. Everyone present had dressed in their most elaborate attire. Couples and single men in evening clothes moved in and out of the service bar area to one end of the hall. Charity accepted a glass of champagne and strolled about, listening to a commentary on the origin and value of the Homestead's considerable inventory. After a scrumptious dinner, Spec took Charity aside, into an elaborate garden behind the building.

Bordered by a sculptured hedge, the formal plot gave an impression of Versailles or Buckingham palace. Charity drew in the heady fragrance of the flowers. Soft moonlight competed with flickering kerosene torches. Spec found a white wrought-iron bench and seated Charity upon it.

"You can have it. The owner has agreed to accept any reasonable offer," Spec told her eagerly.

"I won't do business with a man of mystery. Who is this owner?" Charity demanded.

"Uh—er, yes, well, outside of myself, you're the only one to know. It's Abner Waterford. He's instructed me to inform you that you may have a half interest for a minimal down payment and, I'm afraid, rather large monthly installments until it is paid off. That will be in addition to his usual percentage of the revenue."

"Oh, no it won't. Those monthly payments will include his percentage. What are we talking about in dollars?"

"Ten thousand down and five a month, plus the percentage," Spec informed her.

"We'll talk about that later. But, one way or another, I'm going to have that place."

Three short blasts on the whistle announced the descent of the elevator cage. Hiram Dingle, the shift foreman, and Victor Prentiss, the Vindicator Mine supervisor, stood easy on the shaky platform. Both wore grim expressions. Dingle waited until they had passed the first level before speaking.

"I'm as certain of it as if I saw him at it with my own eyes," Dingle stated.

"I find it hard to believe," Prentiss responded.

"Harry's always been a solid man. He's worked when others joined the unionists."

"Sure. Because he's been linin' his own pockets all the while," Dingle countered. "A high-grading bastard, all smiles and flattery for the ladies, a cheery greeting and tip of his hat to the boss. Considering how long he's worked here, I'd say he could have taken four, five thousand dollars in gold from here."

"That's preposterous," Prentiss stated. "How could he move that much ore?"

"We're in some might rich pockets down on the seventh level. Several places there's free gold in the ore. Harry's been around. The way he works shows that. What he don't know is I found his hidden exit. From the looks of things, he's been takin' it out by the bagfull."

Both men lapsed into silence again as the platform lift slid past the fifth level. With the striking miners rounded up and shipped out of Cripple Creek and the supply of willing workers far less than the demand, the Vindicator was down to two shifts. Now, after midnight, the supervisor and foreman had the place to themselves. Themselves and Harry Orchard, if Dingle was correct. The elevator stopped on the seventh level and Hiram Dingle opened the swing bar in the safety railing.

"Come on, it's this way," Dingle directed.

Pale tunnels of light came from their brass miner's lamps. The carbide gas flames hissed faintly as they burned. Contrary to the opinions of the uninitiated, their footsteps did not echo in the roughly carved passageways. Hiram led the way to a section of the mine never before seen by Victor Prentiss.

"Here it is, Vic. This is what I was tellin' you about."

Bands of dull, leadlike gray and others with a bluish cast ran through the rock. To any but a qualified mining engineer, or a well-experienced miner, these would appear as mere interesting variations. Prentiss gaped in consternation.

"Why . . . why wasn't I told about this?"

"No one knew, until I caught on to Harry's high-gradin'. Believe it or not, *he* sank this side drift and kept it quiet. Most of the work's on fifth level. He could come in here on his off shift and blast when they blasted, haul when they hauled. The end is the same. He makes the money, the mine doesn't."

Victor Prentiss had been listening to a faint hissing sound, only slightly louder and out of sync with the rhythmic pulse of the carbide lamps. He touched Hiram's shoulder and started to point toward the source.

"Hi, what's tha—"

An enormous blast of dynamite flashed whitely and wiped them out of existence before Victor Prentiss could complete the sentence. Rock fell, covering their smashed bodies. A huge billow of dust hurtled toward the open shaft. Rumbles of the explosion chased each other through the many drifts, stopes, and parallels.

"Mine Explosion Kills Two"

Black-bordered headlines filled all the newspapers the next day. Naturally, the Mine Owners Association blamed the striking miners. No one thought of Harry Orchard. Both Prentiss and Dingle had been widely liked in the mining district. Sentiment ran high. Those unionists who had not been deported before received the immediate wrath of the populace.

"Round up every damned one of them," became the motto of the day.

Charity Rose followed the story with grim certainty that she'd chosen her headquarters correctly while she waited for the paperwork to be completed on her acquisition of half interest in the Old Homestead. Timberline arrived, along with her solid man, a hulking giant named P. Klugger. When Charity asked what the initial stood for, neither would give an answer. Timberline gave a simple explanation of his presence.

"The house will need a bouncer. Might as well have one we know is on our side."

The Citizen's Alliance, emboldened by the sudden rush of new members, and encouraged by the Mine Owners Association, decided that every union miner and sympathizer should be driven from the district and never allowed to return.

In order to distinguish those who upheld the status quo, Association men began to wear a white enamel button on their lapels which admonished the miscreants: "You Can Never Come Back!"

Timberline put the entire matter into focus. "All this turmoil is going to affect business."

Charity urged a more optimistic outlook. "Wait and see. Men will come wherever there's work. There are certain things they can't do without. We happen to be in the business of providing one of those."

Chapter 12

Birdsong drifted through the open windows of the Old Homestead. Warming weather produced fresh, pine-scented zephyrs, which blended well with the odors of turpentine, wallpaper paste, and fresh paint. Nothing stimulates optimism like a change of scene. Charity Rose decided to promote enthusiasm in her associates and the public by remodeling the Old Homestead and holding a Grand Opening.

"We want the banquet hall to be light and airy," Charity insisted as she stood with fists on hips, examining the tall, narrow windows. "It's going to cost a bit, but I want to cut into the wall and enlarge some of those windows."

"Where will you get the glass?" Klugger asked. "It's mighty dear in these parts."

"Our, ah, silent partner can see to that. He wants this place to make money, we're going to show him how it's done. But first you have to—"

"I know," Timberline injected. "Spend money to make money. Honey, we've been at this for a week now. The first of the new girls will arrive in two days. What do we do with them?"

"Put 'em to work polishing silver if nothing else," Charity suggested. In a more serious vein she went on. "Having the girls here and idle worries me. Mr. Waterford keeps inquiring into the ages of the girls we've retained and if any of them are real beauties. I know it's customary for the proprietors of a sporting house to sample the merchandise, but I've been hearing a few things about our partner that don't sit right."

"Huh. You're not the only one. Seems he had a real tragic experience some time ago. Folks say he was married once. She ran out on him, took every penny he had. Left him literally out in the street. Worse, she's supposed to have made a lot of public remarks about his poor performance in the bedroom."

Charity frowned. "I'd not heard that. I do know he seems determined to find younger and younger companions. From what more than a couple of reliable sources say, he and Pearl De Vere once had a romantic fling."

"That old coot and Pearl?" Timberline asked skeptically.

"Stranger things have happened," Charity dismissed. "Come on, let's leave this work to the men. I have something I want to show you."

"What's that?" Timberline inquired.

"A little showmanship for the grand opening,"

Charity answered cryptically.

In the comfortable third floor suite Charity had chosen for her own, she produced two boxes from the massive, cherry wood armoir. "Here, these are for you," she explained to Timberline. Gesturing with one box, she added, "These are all the rage in Paris right now."

Excited as only a dedicated clothes horse could be, Timberline tore through the brown wrapping paper and string and opened the box. From the tissue lining she extracted a pair of diamond-spattered, spike-heel shoes. They would, she saw readily, come up to the bottom of her calf. The high heels would make her a good three inches taller.

"Must kill your feet to wear them," the soiled dove observed.

"You'll get used to them. Open the other box."

That turned out to be a new, expensive, and revealingly cut gown that showed off the heels to advantage. Timberline loved it at first look.

"Now, I want you to do your hair up differently, Timberline. Pile it up high, like the ladies of King Louis's court."

"They wore wigs," Timberline pointed out.

"I know. We'll have to make do with your natural tresses, dear. Your hair is long enough and pretty enough to get by."

Timberline produced a pout. Hardly the reaction Charity expected, she asked why. "All of this . . ." Timberline waved a hand at the dress, the spike-heels, and the idea of a new hairdo. "It'll make me look like a giant. I'll never get anything but spanking johns now."

Blank-faced, Charity responded, "If that's what keeps them happy, keep them happy."

Both young women broke into fits of giggles.

Sam Steele glared at the small, rat-faced man in the solitary cell of the Cripple Creek jail. A trickle of blood ran from the corner of the man's mouth, and he sat in a manner that favored the ribs on the right side of his chest. A bright red spot on his forehead would certainly become a large bruise within a short while. Steele massaged the knuckles of his right hand with his other, eyes afire with the desire to hurt and maim.

"Tell me all about it, Joe. How was it done?" Steele demanded.

"I don't know nothin'. I swear it, Mr. Steele. I never learned about powder work. I never knew there was an explosion until the next day."

"C'mon, Joe. The union hired some big-time talent, right? Maybe Al Horsley, eh?"

"There's nothin' I can tell you, Mr. Steele. Honest."

Sam Steele's right fist, protected by a thin, black-leather glove, produced a meaty smack and a slight snapping noise when he hit Joe Galland in the mouth.

Torches blazed outside the Old Homestead on the night of the Grand Opening. Rich carriages and saddle horses filled the stable yard. Some prospective patrons came on foot. Had they been able to move, the walls would have bulged. A string quartet in the banquet hall vied with the tinkling of a piano in the bar. Laughter and surprised shouts rang in the still nocturnal air. A wheel of fortune had been set up, with unique prizes described in graphic detail. Men clamored over each other to risk a ten dollar bill for an opportunity to choose one of the erotic treasures offered on the wheel. As the owner, Charity was not for sale.

Like the grande dame of a Paris salon, she presided over the festivities. Here and there she patted a shoulder or arm, kissed a cheek, or shared a glass of champagne with the exclusively male clientele. The great occasion had begun with a private dinner party for forty of the community's prominent figures. This, in turn, devolved into a riotous night of bacchanal. Before an hour of the glittering gala had passed, Charity spotted two wanted men. Certain they would be using aliases and keep there whereabouts secret, she launched the first of her missions for the tattling tarts.

"Glenda, Melody, those two over here," she informed two of the well-preened doves. "Go work your best wiles on them. Get them into bed and learn all you can about where they are living and what names they use."

"Oooh, are we going to set up a little book for blackmail?" Glenda inquired, eyes hot with avarice.

"Honey, if you think that way, you won't be working here another hour," Charity informed her. "I've good reason to want to know and it's nothing to trouble yourself over. Just do as I say."

Smiling sweetly, Charity moved away with a graceful sway, scattering compliments to the delighted guests. The revelry went even beyond her expectations, and the last customer didn't depart until four in the morning. Exhausted, the entire staff of the Old Homestead made hurried preparations for sleep. Tonight, Charity felt certain, she would not be bothered with nightmares.

Striding through wisps of low-lying cloud, the slender figure in black resembled a spectral wraith fleeing the coming daylight. Before the roosters of Cripple Creek had crowed a second time, C. M. Rose stood at the door to the central police station. Inside a sleepy-eyed desk sergeant glanced up and yawned in the face of the visitor.

"I understand you hold outstanding warrants on Carlisle 'Kid' Raynes and Noah Ellers."

"Um, just a moment, feller," the aging, potbellied sergeant responded. "Names aren't familiar. I'll have to look it up on the log book."

His thick, stubby fingers riffled paper for a while, then stopped at a certain page. He ran the black-rimmed nail of his left index finger down the column there and stopped midway.

"Yep, here's Raynes. Murder and armed robbery. 'Warrant issued by circuit court to Cripple Creek PD,'" he quoted. "That was one month ago. There's a five hundred dollar reward offered by Denver and Rio Grande Railroad, also. Paperwork is all here. Lemme see if I find the other."

After another short search, the sergeant nodded and read aloud again. " 'Noah Ellers, wanted for armed robbery of a stage coach, attempted murder and mayhem. Warrant issued on complaint of Wells Fargo and Company. Five hundred dollars reward.' There they are, young man. What do you want to know about them?"

"I'd be happy to serve those warrants for you," Charity responded.

"You mean today?" the startled policeman asked.

"I mean right now. This minute. I'd like the papers and the loan of a mounted police officer. Raynes is holed up some distance outside town."

"Say, you're serious, ain't ya? What give you the idea to go after them fellers?"

Charity produced her badge from Dos Cabezas. "I'm a special deputy, Graham County, Arizona Territory. For want of a better description, a bounty hunter. I intend to collect their scalps before they move on."

"And good luck to you. Kid Raynes is bad business from any way you look. Mounted men don't come on until day shift at seven-thirty. Don't know that the chief would lend you one, though."

"What about one on his day off?" Charity prompted.

"Hummm. Now that might work. There's Cliff Collins. He's got today an' tomorrow off."

"Where will I find him, sergeant?" Charity asked.

"Home most likely. Got him a nice young wife. If he ain't too tired out, if you know what I mean, he'd be glad to go along. You'd have to give him a share in the rewards, of course."

"Naturally. That's no hardship for me, sergeant. How do I find his home?"

The sergeant gave directions and Charity headed for Lattimer Street. Cliff Collins turned out to be an affable man with curly hair, a broad rump, and a tendency toward a paunch. The last two Charity attributed to his riding his beat instead of walking it. Contrary to the sergeant's salacious suggestion, Charity found him up, dressed in casual clothes and finishing breakfast. He listened to only two sentences before bursting out.

"Will I? You bet I'll go. Uh, I don't mean to sound greedy or anything, but would there be a share in any rewards?"

"I thought it over and decided to offer you a seventy-thirty split. There's a thousand dollars total at stake, so that might fatten your bank account a little."

"Fatten it, hell. It'll allow me to open one for the first time."

"Then let's get started."

"Who do we go after first?" Cliff asked.

"Noah Ellers. He's right here in town. Staying at the Harmony House."

"Cliff, sweetheart, it sounds dangerous," the big-eyed comely young wife injected.

"No more than my ever'day job. Not since the miners went on the rampage, honey," Cliff responded, rising. "Let me get my gun and we'll go, Mr. Rose," he said over his shoulder to Charity.

With a reverberating bang the door slammed inward. Bleary-eyed and hungover, Noah Ellers sat up in bed to stare into the muzzle of a Colt's Bisley revolver. Instinctively his hand twitched and started to reach toward a six-gun on the nighttable.

"Don't," a husky voice advised. "Unless you want to wake up next in hell."

"Whaddya want? I ain't got no money," Ellers croaked weakly.

"Noah Ellers, alias Tom Howard? I have a warrant for your arrest," Charity informed the wanted man.

"Oh, shit," Ellers muttered.

"That was mighty damn easy, C. M.," Cliff Collins remarked half an hour later. They had booked the prisoner into jail and were headed now to the livery stable.

"Don't count on the next one going so smoothly," Charity cautioned. "Kid Raynes is young, tough, and a bit crazy."

"Who'd he kill?" Cliff inquired.

"His father, who was an express car clerk on the Denver and Rio Grande, and a half-brother he'd brought along on the robbery. The way the Pinkertons figured it, he didn't want to share the loot. The half-brother was only thirteen."

"And we're going to take him by ourselves?" Cliff gulped.

"No. *I'm* going to take him, you're going to back me up," Charity clarified.

Kid Raynes heard the clop of approaching horses long before he saw the animals. Crafty and cruel, the nineteen-year-old punk affected a sarcastic snarl to his lips and drew farther back in the concealing brush around the small cave he used for a hideout. It might be his best—and only—friend, Butch Thompson from Leadville, come to bring him supplies. But the Kid doubted that. Butch was only fourteen and considered by most to be somewhat of a sissy. That didn't matter to the Kid. *They* knew, he and Butch, what their friendship was all about. His doubts had to do with Butch's age. Being that young, he didn't think Butch could get away from home for very long. Though the Kid had run away at twelve, Butch was different. Sensitive and easily hurt might be the way to describe it. The Kid saw a horse's head, then another.

Only no people. A cold chill grabbed at Kid Raynes's vitals. He was being hunted, and by someone well skilled in the art of stalking men. He slid the hinge-framed Smith & Wesson American out of leather and eared back the hammer. How would they come for him? From which direction? Did they know where he was?

Crrrrick! No further than a few feet away the ratcheting of the sear notches on a Colt hammer paralyzed the Kid for a vital second. Then, reflexively, he fired in the direction of the sound. A deep-throated grunt followed the echoing report. Then a man's voice, attempting to be quiet.

"Damn. Oh, damn that hurts."

Reprieve swelled through the Kid's breast. With one opponent down he had a chance. The Kid came to his feet, knocked the cut brush aside from the front of his cave and made a dash for his horse. He covered thirty yards safely when a bullet cracked past his ear and smacked into an amber blob of pitch on a pine truck. He heard the sound of the shot before the bullet struck.

"The next one goes in the back of your head," a husky voice informed the Kid.

Where had he heard that voice before? Kid Raynes pondered it as he dived forward to the ground. Another round burned air over his head. Fear ate at his guts and tears pooled in his eyes. Shit! He hadn't cried since the first night after he ran away from home. He'd shown them, though. He'd come back and killed his brutal, hard-drinking old man and his sniveling coward of a half-brother. Made a good haul, too. A rustle of brush told him that his hunter was on the move.

Up and away, Kid Raynes made it within five feet of his horse when a terrible, white-hot pain exploded in his right leg. He plowed face first into the damp pine needles. Self-preservation drove him to roll to one side and bring his Smith American into play.

His bullet knocked the hat from a slim, dark-garbed figure a moment before someone punched him in the chest with a sledgehammer. At least the numbing impact of the .45 slug felt that way at first. All of a sudden the big Smith became too heavy to hold up. And something had happened to his vision. Was he really seeing a girl bending over him?

No. Her face blurred, became indistinct and

wavering. Tears squeezed out of his eyes and new agony wracked his body.

"Oh, it hurts so awfully," Kid Raynes heard himself say as if from a mile away.

"Tell that to your little brother, you son of a bitch," Charity Rose barked.

Quickly she recovered his six-gun and hunted up her hat. Long auburn hair tucked safely out of sight she went to aid Cliff Collins. He sat with his back against a boulder. With both hands he held shut the entry wound.

"I was lucky," the young policeman informed her. "It didn't hit the artery. I'll be sore as hell for a while, though."

"You should have cocked your weapon right after you got off your horse," Charity advised him.

"Police training says never to do that," Cliff protested.

"Mounted policemen in fair-sized cities don't often go after cold-blooded killers. Out here you'll soon find that keeping alive and unharmed comes first and following someone's rules is way down the list. Tell you what I'll do, Cliff. When we sell the Kid's things you can use the money for a doctor. Now let's patch that up enough to get into town."

"What about the Kid?" Cliff inquired.

"He'll be going into town over the saddle, not upright in it," Charity told him simply.

"You're a mighty fine partner, C. M. Ain't many men good as you, I guess."

Unaccountably, to Cliff Collins's way of things,

the young bounty hunter blushed fleetingly. "That's a bigger compliment than you thought, Cliff," the bounty collector said sincerely.

Chapter 13

Rumor mills, even when separated by considerable distance, seem to feed on the same grist. It began in Denver, but soon the talk of the whole district centered on how the mysterious C. M. Rose was actually a woman. The wives discussed it first, vicariously sharing a supposed adventurous life, then the men began to remark upon the possibility.

Yet, C. M. Rose had such a reputation for speed, from the arrest of Kelly in Creede, and for toughness, from the capture of Noah Ellers and bringing in Kid Raynes, that none wished to challenge the question openly. Likewise, no one connected the deadly gunfighter with the lovely new madam of the Old Homestead. For three days Cripple Creek buzzed with versions of Cliff Collins's account of the deeds of C. M. Rose. One person in particular had a greater interest than the others. The glittering, mad eyes of Norbert Klinger followed Rose from the shadows of buildings and alleyways.

He watched as the bounty hunter rode out of town. He trailed along, observed the transformation and verified his jumbled perceptions from the time of his arrest. Then, filled with a mounting frenzy of kill lust, he shadowed Miss Charity Rose back to the Old Homestead.

Harry Orchard seethed as he listened to his contact, Abe Larner. "It's not my doin', mind you," Larner reported. "McRoberts exerted influence on the members o' the Free Coinage Union as well as our own people in the Western Federation of Miners."

"You mean that's it? One man with a big mouth and no pay for a job well done?"

"That's the substance of it, Al—er—Harry. McRoberts pointed out that the Vindicator blast was unauthorized and reminded everyone of the negative results it has had. Our agreement was that you cleared everything before doing it."

"Our agreement," Harry said heatedly, "was that I come over here and crush the strikebreakers. That's the only way to get the mine owners to sit down and discuss issues. The hows and whys of my trade are my own business."

"I'm sorry, Harry. McRoberts doesn't see it that

way, and now neither does the membership."

After Larner departed, Harry's bitterness spilled over. He struck his wife for the first time, shouted at the kids and stalked out of the house. Hands sunk in the pockets of his canvas miner's trousers, he walked past the baseball diamond without even a sideward glance. Later he met by prearrangement with a dapper little man he knew as a detective for the Florence and Cripple Creek Railroad.

"These are the men, best as I know," Harry informed the investigator. "Their overall leader is Angus McRoberts. He's a bad one." He handed over a list. "Using that cowardly infernal machine at the Vindicator was the last straw. No way I could keep quiet about men who would stoop to such a thing." Harry had carefully omitted Abe Larner.

"Hummmm. A good job of work, Orchard. I've been authorized to pay you a regular sum to keep your ears and eyes open for us. No matter how many times it's been tried, we haven't been able to get rid of all the strikers as yet. With a little help from you, we might wrap this up rather soon. Keep at it."

"You bet, Mister, ah, Jones," Harry replied, mind working on what new skulduggery he could lay at the feet of those who had betrayed him.

A bell tinkled mutedly when Charity Rose entered the mortuary establishment of Fairley Brothers and Lampman's. The entryway, she noted, was so inviting that it could have graced the home of any moderately well-to-do family. A gigantic fern hung down from an iron stand in the sunny front window. Her feet trod on a green Brussles carpet. Comfortable chairs, showing no wear for all the frequent use, were scattered around the anteroom. Situated before a door that must connect to a central hallway, a large mahogany desk created a barrier. Charity stopped there. A mement later, when no one appeared, she gave closer examination to the room.

A large glass case on a sturdy table caught Charity's eye. It contained a collection of catalogued exhibits, much like a museum. She quickly discovered that these were momentos of people who had met violent death in Cripple Creek and been laid out at this establishment.

There was a lunch bucket of a miner who had been struck by lightning, side combs of Two-go Ruby, a soiled dove who had swallowed strychnine. Also the pistol of a gambler who shot himself through the mouth, a piece of fuse that another had used to blow off his head with dynamite, each with its neatly typewritten label. Among them Charity found a lock of Pearl De Vere's red hair. Reminded of the purpose of her visit, she turned away as one of the morticians stepped through the doorway behind the desk.

Fittingly dressed in a conservative, plain black suit, he had a pallor and aura suggesting that which lay beyond the grave. "May I help you?"

Charity turned on her sweetest smile. "Why, yes. I have some questions I'd like to ask you."

"Concerning a recently departed?" he asked in solemn, hollow tones.

"Oh, no. Ah, rather yes. About Pearl De Vere," Charity blundered.

The undertaker produced a pained, somewhat bored expression. "We've been asked I don't know how many times. Yes, Miss De Vere dyed her hair."

"Ummm, that's not exactly what I wanted to inquire about. When you were, ah, preparing her for her laying out, did you happen to notice any particularly outstanding scars or marks?"

Eyebrows shot toward the dark hairline. "How unusual that you should ask. Poor Miss De Vere must have had some sort of terrible accident in her past. Her, ah, person was a mass of scar tissue. Quite out of the ordinary for a lady."

Charity's green eyes glowed with triumph. It added another small piece to her building theory. "You've been most kind. Thank you. Would you have any way of judging the age of the most recent scars?"

"Oh, at least five years or more."

That fit with the time Pearl set up her bordello. A nice piece of detective work, Charity congratulated herself. "I won't trouble you longer. I assure you what you revealed will remain confidential. Perhaps I might offer you a small token of my appreciation."

Charity delved into her clutch purse and produced twenty-five Old Homestead wooden dollars. "I'm sure you can find a means to make use of these."

Her informant glanced at the objects in the palm of his hand and smiled fleetingly. "I do believe I shall. You're . . . you're Miss Charity Carver who bought out the Homestead, right?"

"That I am. Good day to you, sir."

With further avenues of conversation shut off by Charity's retreating back, the mortician remained silent.

Among those at the top of Sam Steele's list were the union organizers who had so far evaded deportation. When word reached him that there was to be a gathering of unionists in the back room of the El Paso Club, he quickly gathered his bully-boys and marched on the saloon. News of their approach reached the gentlemen in question by an unexpected source.

Harry Orchard, known as a strikebreaker since his return to the Vindicator six weeks earlier, brought the warning. It enabled the leaders to escape. The rank and file remained in rowdy conclave to provide a diversion. Which also trapped Harry when the doors banged open and windows shattered to reveal Steele and his "deputies."

"Nobody moves," Sam Steele snarled. "And I want to see a show of empty hands."

"Damn ya all an' the bloody-handed tyrants ye work for," one cocky miner replied.

"Come on in, boys," Steele commanded. "Let's see who we've got here."

One by one the miners were identified and sent outside to form up for the now-familiar march to the depot. When Steele came to Harry Orchard, he stared long and thoughtfully. Fairly certain of his conclusion, Steele signaled for his men to start off with the deportees.

"I'm keepin' this one for special questioning," Steele announced.

"Ya see?" a surly miner complained. "It was that damn turncoat Orchard all the time."

"Now then," Steele said after the others were out of hearing range. "If I'm not mistaken, you're Albert Horsley. Orchard's just a name of convenience, eh?"

"I've got nothing to say to you," Harry came back defiantly.

"Oh, I think you will. I could ship you back to Idaho and let them hang you. Or, considering the method used, I could hold you for prosecution in the Vindicator explosion."

This put a new light on matters for Harry Orchard. A slight nervous tic developed at the outer corner of his left eye. "Look, it—it may be that I'm this Albert Horsley. But I want you to know I've reformed. I'm married and have a family now. I've been working during the strike and I have nothing to do with the strikers. You heard what that man said. They even suspected me when I came here."

"You're the one who warned them, eh? Well, Horsley or Orchard, that don't make it sound like you've reformed as much as you'd like me to believe."

"I had a good reason for it. I'm working fulltime as an informer for the Florence and Cripple Creek. They wanted me to get close to the miners and find out where the big shots would be. Telling the miners about your raid seemed a good way to gain their confidence."

Steele looked doubtful. "That's quite a story you've told. Still, I think it should be checked out. I'm going to hold you in jail for a while and see what we can learn."

"But, I . . ."

"Oh, there's also the question of the bomb meant for Mr. Waterford. Don't press too hard, Horsley," Steele advised him.

The hours of darkness passed slowly for Harry Orchard. He worried over whether or not the railroad people would acknowledge his involvement with their detectives, what his wife would say or do if questioned by Steele. Through it all hung the spectre of the hangman's noose if he did get sent back to Idaho, or got convicted of the Vindicator blast. By the time dawn paled the sky, Harry reached a state of exhaustion, yet his frayed nerves kept him keyed up to the point of fitful pacing in the single cell at the jail.

"I've got something for you." Good news arrived with the turnkey, who also brought Harry some breakfast and a steaming mug of coffee. The heavily laden tray of glazed stonewear slid through a slot in the cell door.

"What's that? Did Steele croak over night?" Harry groused.

"Not at all. He wants you to get straightened up after you have breakfast. Then he wants to talk with you again."

"Fine by me," Harry said with mock indifference.

Sam Steele looked up from his desk and nodded perfunctorily when Harry Orchard entered the outer office. "Did you enjoy your breakfast? It's the last one you're gonna get on the County."

Hope brightened Harry's face. "How do you mean that?"

"I'm turning you loose, Horsley. Your story checked out with the Florence and Cripple Creek people. Which makes me think that as a railroad man you'd not be the one to pull the Vindicator deal. Watch yourself close, though, because I'll be dogging your steps from now on."

"I'm obliged to you, Mr. Steele," Harry said, heady with the first draught of the air of freedom.

Steele had to acknowledge to himself that other factors influenced his decision. He knew what it meant to be a wanted man. He was wanted a few places himself, like Wyoming and Montana. That being the case, he'd not send Horsley back. He would never stoop to bounty hunting, for like most men with a price on his head, he considered them the scum of the earth. Even so, with Horsley around, it made his job more difficult. If only he could get something solid on the man.

With most of the strikers removed from the district and the remaining leaders on the run, the mines began to operate as usual. Which made money flow through the communities once more. The Old Homestead enjoyed an unusually big night for midweek. Lights spilled from the windows and music tinkled from the bar and banquet room. Men suddenly flush with money, and a few merchants cheating on their wives, filled the establishment. Abner Waterford put in an appearance at ten o'clock, at the height of festivities. With him he brought the pretty little blonde, whom he introduced as Louanne Fletcher, who had so far remained steadfast to her commitment.

After obtaining refreshments, Abner zeroed in on one of Charity's more nubile recruits, oblivious to the humiliation it caused his companion. All the while, the millionaire hovered over his attractive new partner. Charity had not yet put in an appearance, choosing to observe the activities in the drawing room and bar from a prepared cubbyhole that gave access to both. It took only moments for her interest to center on Abner Waterford.

"Has anyone told you that your eyes are like a high mountain sky?" Abner drawled to the youthful prostitute he had latched onto.

Only about a hundred times since I came here, she thought with boredom. "Why, no honey-pot. You have the quaintest way of saying things," she said aloud.

"My glass is empty," Louanne said in a tiny voice, afraid of angering Waterford, yet needing the pain-numbing effect of the liquor.

Waterford ignored her. Charity could see the effects of earlier drinking on the wealthy tycoon. He weaved slightly, even while sitting, and slurred his words. Cloe, the young hooker, seemed frightened, and the older women quite obviously were please to avoid Waterford's attentions. The fear that Louanne radiated came across clearly to Charity. She sent for Timberline and Klugger.

"We have a chance to find out a few things about our silent partner," she began. Quickly she briefed them on what to do.

Ten minutes later, Charity made her grand entrance. Voices stilled and all male eyes turned to the lovely young woman who seemed to float above the treads as she descended the staircase. She went directly to Abner Waterford's table. Abner made a big show of standing at her approach, in a parody of fine manners. He made a flowery obeisance to Charity's beauty, yet his deep-set eyes glittered with a hatred that he could not distinguish from love.

While he went through his public show, Timberline slipped up to Abner's new girl and led her and Louanne out of the room. Charity picked up on Abner's insincere flattery and chattered away to provide a distraction.

"I do declare, Abner, you're a regular old flatterer. 'Finest flower of fair womanhood,' indeed. You certainly know how to turn a girl's head. It's such a pleasure to have you visit our humble establishment." She cast a sidelong glance to be sure Timberline had escaped with the soiled dove Abner had been lionizing. "I hope you found everything to your satisfaction."

"Oh, I have. Indeed I have. Tell me, what is the average age of the young ladies in your employ?" Waterford pried.

Charity wrinkled her pretty brow. "Nineteen I would say. Perhaps twenty."

Waterford looked disappointed. "Then I gather this, ah, treasure is your youngest?" Abner's brow furrowed when he was unable to locate Cloe. He showed no sign of pique over the departure of Louanne Fletcher.

"Oh, no. We have one girl much younger," Charity invented. "She's only fourteen and not working at the, ah, trade. She's from a troubled home with a brutal father," she continued at Waterford's heightened interest. "She knows what our business is all about and has expressed a willingness to earn her own way. As a matter of fact, there's been a couple of times . . . ah, there I go, telling tales out of school. I *do* tend to ramble."

"Oh, no, that's quite all right. I'm concerned about the welfare of all our, er, charges. Do go on."

"In that case," Charity went on, lying smoothly. "On one occasion we caught her and our cleanup and towel boy, Jason, experimenting somewhat clumsily in a closet. It seems Jason had never experienced such delights before, and Penny undertook to initiate him. The other time she actually stole an older man away from one of the working girls. She had him up in her room before Klugger arrived in time to prevent any wrongdoing. That's when we found out . . ." Charity coyly lowered her lashes. She could almost hear Waterford panting with anticipation.

"We found that Penny's homelife had not been at all proper. It turned out that in addition to beating his five children, her father robbed Penny of her innocence. We felt it necessary to keep a tight rein on Penny until she reaches a more acceptable age."

"You, uh, did the right thing," Waterford said, almost slobbering. "I'd like to, ah, meet this girl, have a talk with her. Maybe I could help straighten her out."

"That would be most kind of you, Abner. We'll see about it . . . someday. Now, let me tell you how handsome you are in that suit. Pearl gray is definitely your color."

For the next twenty minutes Charity flirted

shamelessly with Abner, then excused herself to answer an urgent call. Instead of heading to the downstairs toilet, she hurried to her private suite. She found a horrified Timberline examining the hideously scarred body of the once lovely little blonde, Louanne.

"That does it. I'd had my doubts before. Then what I learned about Pearl left little room. Come, dear, I'll help you get dressed," she directed to the frightened girl.

"Y-you're not going to say anything to Abner are you? Oh, please don't," Louanne begged.

"I have some rather specific plans for Abner now," Charity said grimly.

Eyes rolling, the girl became hysterical. "You can't! Don't you see, it'll ruin everything."

"What are you talking about? We'll protect you, give you sanctuary here at the Homestead if need be," Charity responded.

"That'll ruin everything. He'll take it out on Davey," Louanne cried.

"Who's Davey?" Charity asked.

"My son. He's only seven. I agreed to do Abner's bidding in all things for a period of one year. In exchange, he gives me an annual stipened for the rest of my life and he'll put Davey through college."

Astonished, Charity pointed to her disfigured body. "Y-you mean you put yourself through this in exchange for so little?"

"*It's not so little,* not if you come from a background like mine. We've always been poor. Dirt poor. My Paw had forty acres of hillside rocks to farm. Davey an' me, we were just another burden. I left Tennessee and took Davey along. We settled in Denver. Then Abner, Mr. Waterford, found me." Louanne began to sob.

Charity placed an arm around her bare shoulders. "There, there, Louanne. We can still help you. Trust in what I say."

"What for? It's not so bad now. Abner no longer finds me stimulating, except for the kind of degrading exhibit he put me through downstairs. I've only a month to go on my contract. Don't you see? If I breach it now, all my pain and suffering will have been for nothing." Suddenly she blanched. "In fact, there's a secrecy clause. If Abner learns what I've told you, he'll turn me 'n' Davey out with nothing."

"Why that bastard," Charity blurted her anger. "How can any man be so low? Oh, I know all about how he was supposed to have been done dirt by a woman long ago. Nothing excuses this kind of vileness. Somehow, someway, he's got to be made to pay for what he's done to women ever since. Outright killing's too good for him. I'll think of something, Louanne, don't you worry." She rose from the girl's side and crossed to the door.

"Timberline, help Louanne compose herself. Get her dressed, freshen her up and bring her back downstairs. And Louanne, don't you worry. Abner will never learn about what happened up here, no matter how long he lives."

Chapter 14

Moths and other night-flying insects fluttered at the windows of the Old Homestead when Charity rejoined the revelers in the drawing room. Abner Waterford had ordered champagne, and the late shift from the mines had cleaned up and dropped in for some hearty recreation. Charity fixed a big, artificial smile on her face and twined an arm around Abner's neck.

"Abner, I'm simply famished. I ran into Louanne in the ladies' room and she's starving also. Be a real dear and order up a late dinner for the three of us?"

"Well, I, er . . . of course. Why not?" Visibly aroused by Charity's familiarity, Waterford summoned the waiter. He quickly outlined his seven-course idea of a late night repast. While he did, Louanne returned, looking much better.

"Abner, you're such an old darling," Charity

simpered. "When are you going to dance with me?"

Waterford blinked owlishly. "What's wrong with right now?"

"I'd be delighted," Charity burbled.

On the small area of cleared floor, bare for dancing, Charity pressed herself tightly against Abner's body. She soon became aware of his slow arousal. Deliberately she ground her pubic arch into him and he groaned audibly. The long fingernails of her left hand toyed with the sensitive region of his neck. When the number ended, Abner walked back to the table bent slightly forward in an attempt to conceal his throbbing erection.

"Oh, they've brought our oysters," Charity trilled. Actually she thought raw oysters were horrible. Those slimy gray lumps somehow intimidated her.

Their dinner progressed and Charity made sure Abner's glass remained filled. After dessert, baked apples, Charity got the millionaire out on the dance floor again. Two numbers in a row had him fairly panting with lust and reeling from all the drink he had consumed. On tiptoe, Charity whispered into his ear.

"We can have a lot more fun if you come back sometime without that insipid little blonde."

Abner smacked his lips. "What, ah, sort of, er, fun did you have in mind?"

"The kind you have without clothes," she goaded. "I might even . . . include Penny in the party with us."

"Gaaaah!" Abner gagged and nearly discharged in his underdrawers. "Make that tonight. I can send Louanne to the hotel in a cab. We'll have the whole night. You an' me, an' little Penny."

"No, not tonight. Just looking at that baggage you brought along turns me cold. I couldn't enjoy it, knowing . . . knowing you had a yen for her while being with me."

"What can I say? What can I offer? I'll do *anything* if you relent. Think of the joy we could have. You and Penny and me."

"I'm afraid we can't. Not tonight."

"Then wha' abou' th' pretty one I talked to earlier? Wha' 'bout her, huh?"

"I've given her and Klugger the night off to go to a dinner and social over to Creede."

"Damn him for taking my woman," Abner declared, forgetting that the pair had been present no more than an hour earlier. "I want this Klugger made an example of. I'm firing him for insubordination. Tell him in the morning."

"No way I'll do that. Our contract calls for me to run the place. That means I do the hiring *and* the firing."

"I'll give ya a hunnard fif'y thousan' dollars for your half in'rest."

"My mother never raised any stupid kids, Abner. I'll not sell for that price."

"Yer all alike. Damn women," Abner growled. Passion or not, he walked off from Charity, leaving her alone on the dance floor. He sent his blonde away and sat alone, knocking down stiff shots of whiskey until he neatly inclined forward and passed out with his head on the table. The imposing Timberline showed up and hoisted Waterford over one shoulder. Walking with ease, she delivered him to an empty bed, then turned in, herself.

Abe Larner and the remaining union bosses wanted action. With Angus McRoberts and the more sensible leaders exported due to the information provided by Harry Orchard, the situation had become desperate. Unaware that the very man they employed to eliminate the strikebreakers was responsible for their dilemma, Larner went to Orchard with a new assignment.

"This will be your biggest job so far. The damned scabs at the Findley all take the train from the station in Independence to their hovels in the camps. If you blow that place you can get a whole lot of 'em. Oughtta send the survivors packing right smart."

Leery after his brush with the law, Harry eyed Larner skeptically. "There'll be a powerful stink over something like that. I want my pay in advance."

"Now, Albert . . ."

"Don't you now Albert me. The money first, or no job."

Grudgingly Larner agreed. Early on the morning of June fifth, Harry mentioned to a couple of neighbors that he and John Neville were gong fishing. John, a bartender, had hired a wagon and team, and the pair, Harry maintained, were going to take in the brooks around Love. Since John was a real fanatic at fishing, Harry laughingly told them that he was taking along an extra horse in case he got tired of it and wanted to come home. Accustomed to Harry's unorthodox ways, no one thought a thing of it. With his alibi in place, Harry set off for his most important enterprise.

Along with him and Neville came Steve Adams. They reached Independence after dark. Neville stayed with the wagon at the cutoff. Harry and Steve approached the darkened depot by a roundabout course. There they placed a hundred pound charge of dynamite under the depot platform. They worked in silence, afraid the least sound might betray them. Uncharacteristically, Harry began to worry as they completed their task.

All that's left is the bottle of sulfuric acid, Harry thought tensely. God, if this goes wrong . . . He nearly dropped the open bottle when Steve flopped down a coil of wire. Recovering, Harry fastened the open bottle in a harness which hung from the beam above the explosives. Next he fixed the end of the wire to it. Moving crablike across the ground, he and Steve unwound the wire cautiously until they came to abandoned Delmonico Shaft. There they sat on the dump and waited for the graveyard shift miners to come down from the Findley to catch the owl train to their shacks. Three hundred feet of wire separated them from their murderous device. It was a clear night with a waning moon.

The excellent visibility soon let them see lanterns flashing, and Harry knew that the men had started down the hill. Beyond, on the lower slope of Battle Mountain, a few lamps flickered in the sleeping town of Victor. Icy chills assailed Harry as a dog took up a frantic yapping somewhere. Suddenly he and Steve froze, then flattened against the dump tailings when the headlight of a switch engine at the Portland and Strong mine glared directly at them. By then, a few of the strikebreakers had already reached the depot and milled about on the platform.

"Hang on, Harry," Steve urged in a low whisper. "There'll be more shortly. If we're lucky, there'll be at least forty more from the Shurtleff comin', too."

With what Harry estimated to be only ten or fifteen minutes left to wait, the unexpected intervened to nearly shatter his nerve. A train whistle sounded, echoes bounced off the hillsides, and the strong beam of the headlight wobbled into empty space beyond the curve, not six hundred feet from the depot. Harry lost it. He felt jittery and confusion kept his thoughts swimming. His hands shook so violently that he could hardly pick up the wire.

"Don't pull yet, you goddamned fool!" Steve whispered harshly. "Another second and we'll wipe out the train and every bastard scab on the hill."

Too late. Harry's quaking fingers had already jerked the wire. What had been the depot turned into a white ball that expanded outward, then shrank rapidly to a dull orange glow and the yellow flicker of flames. A deafening roar followed, then splintered boards and random rocks began to fall around them. Harry in the lead, they stumbled and fell several times while they tried to reach their horses tied to trees two hundred feet away. Despite his ringing ears, Harry believed he heard men groaning and women screaming coming from the direction where the depot used to be. The haunting voices never left him all the way to the Cripple Creek cutoff where Neville waited with the wagon.

Excitement tinged Timberline's cheeks when she rushed in to greet Charity. "Did you hear? It's the most awful thing yet. That Western Federation of Miners bunch has gone completely mad. They blew up the Independence railroad depot last night."

A chill passed over Charity. "Did they catch the men who did it?" she asked hopefully.

"No. No one has been accused as yet," Timberline told her.

A sick, hollow feeling of guilt spread inside Charity. In pursuit of other things she had let go too long on a vital clue. Albert Horsley. It had to be him. She had a lead to the notorious bomber, yet had done nothing about it. She would correct that error if she could. If she had time. No doubt, she thought sadly, he would be well on his way out of Colorado. Whether he did or not, there was plenty else to do and a new day to undertake it.

"What else has happened?" she asked Timberline.

"The governor has declared martial law in the district. State troops are on the way. There's to be a mass meeting downtown this afternoon. People are hoppin' mad, even a lot who sympathized with the union. A lawyer fellow is going to talk to folks about what happened and what needs be done. Are you going?"

"I, ah, think not," Charity responded over the rim of her delicate bone china coffee cup. "Our business is here. With the politicians drawing everyone to town, we'll be wise to open early. There's a lot of men who will get their bellies full of harangues before two in the afternoon and be looking for a cool beer or a warm girl."

Charity did not attend the emotion-fraught afternoon's events, but C. M. Rose did. Garbed in black costume, the bounty hunter found a place of vantage and looked over the crowd. One could never tell. Perhaps Horsley was depraved enough to come in and listen to the invective against what could only be termed anonymous murderers. She learned that Clarence Hamlin, a fiery-tempered attorney for the Mine Owners Association, was the lawyer Timberline referred to. He had been chosen to whip up the expected throng.

Noted for his fiery oratory in court, Hamlin had his eye on a political career. He had a strong, resonant voice, which seemed too big for his slight stature and was noted statewide for his gift of oratory. His one great fault was his intemperance, both in habit and speech. Having witnessed impromptu performances by Hamlin at the Old Homestead, Charity considered him a dangerous choice.

Hundreds of angry, determined people gathered by the time Hamlin took his place on the improvised platform. He warmed up his audience with a straight presentation of the facts, as known, of the events at Independence, then moved into his central theme.

"Not only did the powerful blast break every window in Independence, it shattered glass and shook buildings in Victor. Women and children were terrified. Many knew the dark, ominous meaning of such an explosion. Those not already widowed by the murders of the union trembled with fear."

Hamlin teetered back and forth, like a cattail in a windstorm. Unsteady on his feet from his own warm-up with John Barleycorn, he paced unevenly as he spoke and often came dangerously close to the edge of the rough planks that supported him. Shouting and gesticulating, he pleaded to the crowd for men of courage to come forth and avenge the terrible crime.

"Men sundered by that awful blast cry for revenge. Widows and orphaned children, equally victims of this tragedy, wail in their desolated homes for vengeance."

Faces in the crowd grew tense. Men whipped to

fire-eyed fury expected the flamboyant orator to tell them how to achieve that revenge. Applause and calls of encouragement almost drowned out Hamlin's words.

"The sword of justice had been given into our hands," Hamlin proclaimed. "Let us take it forth to conqu—" His voice cut off between syllables as a defiant shot zipped through the air.

Sheriff's deputy Jim Warford acted faster than any man present in the next split second. Launching from his position to one side of the platform, he grabbed Clarence Hamlin and yanked him down. There was no question, not a doubt in anyone's mind. A drifting smoke cloud pinpointed the origin of the shot. It came from Union Hall.

Bullets began to fly in every direction. Glass shattered in the union's bastion and the walls became scarred with hot lead. Two innocent bystanders died, victims of anonymous bullets. The crowd went wild, became a mob. The state troops, having arrived only an hour before, went quickly, if unprepared, into action.

They surrounded Union Hall. Their presence silenced the snipers within. Such quick action far from satisfied the blood lust of the raging citizens. Shouting improvised slogans of anti-union sentiment, they spread out through town. Their frenzy extended through the entire district within an hour.

They raided union stores where supplies of food and clothing were kept for the strikers, scattering the damaged goods in the streets. At once, without fanfare or pretense of legality, the deportations began again. Total chaos, worse than anything the Western Federation of Miners could have conceived, spread like wildfire. While daylight still claimed the Colorado mountains, homes were broken into and families torn apart. Even those who had only been known as friends of union members were classed as undesirables.

By nightfall, only partial order had been restored by the troops. Only the Old Homestead and other pleasure palaces along Meyers Street provided islands of uneasy tranquility under the ready eight-gauge shotguns of P. Klugger and his counterparts. Business, other than the sale of food and drink, suffered considerably. C. M. Rose had ample work. Charity picked out five more wanted men and noted their activities. When the time came, she intended to collect on their bounties. She also reminded herself of the rewards on Steele and promised herself the day would come when he would be unprotected by his badge.

Kept constantly busy in the ongoing turmoil, the town constable and his five policemen did not need another prisoner. When C. M. Rose walked into the constabulary office with *two* prisoners, patience drained to a dangerous low.

"What are you bringing them here for?" Walter Curtis demanded.

"They are wanted men," Charity told the constable simply. "They need to be held somewhere until they can be transported to Denver. Here are arrest warrants on both men from the Denver court, issued on complaint by the police department."

Curtis looked like a man suffering constipation. "Those militia are bringing in men faster than we can shovel 'em onto trains out of here. What am I supposed to do?"

"Put them into a cell," C. M. Rose replied. "I have three more to round up. After all, every criminal we take off the streets hastens a return to normal conditions, right?"

The bounty hunter had him there, Curtis had to admit to himself. He summoned the jailer and had them booked. Charity filled out her reports and left quietly. It appeared that one of the wanted men she recognized ran with the miners. A gunman with a heavy reputation, she wanted to take him when he had the least support. Walking toward the Busted Flush Saloon, Charity considered her strategy.

Normally, with Butch along, she would go through the front door. Today she decided upon a side entrance that admitted persons to a private card room. When she reached her goal, Charity paused to loosen both Bisleys in their holsters. Then she drew the right one and revolved the cylinder until she could insert a fresh cartridge in the sixth chamber. Left hand on the knob, she turned gently and opened the door wide enough to see the interior.

Tenseness flowed out of her when she found the room empty. With short, quiet strides she crossed to the bead curtain that separated the private cubical from the barroom. Her man stood at the bar, his back to her.

Red Cranston had bested seven men in face-on gunfights. He was reputed to have killed at least a dozen more in less straightforward ways. According to his notorious status, Charity held the Bisley steady in her right hand as she stepped through the hanging strings of beads. The sound of the hammer ratcheting back brought instant silence to the room. Cranston's long, scrawny neck flushed scarlet.

"Red Cranston," her husky voice called out. "I have a warrant for your arrest. If you will come along peacefully, rest your hands on the bar while I approach."

"Ain't . . . no way I'm . . . gonna . . ." Cranston fell off to the side, fast as a stone as he spoke. Twisting, he wrenched his six-gun from leather and cocked it before he hit the sawdust-covered floor. Instantly he fired.

Cranston's bullet cracked past close enough to Charity's cheek to be felt. She had fired a fraction of a second before him. Her slug plowed through the space previously occupied by her target's midsection. It gouged out a long trough of hair, scalp, and bone from the top of Red Cranston's head. Stunned into unconsciousness, which proved a merciful death, Cranston's reflexive second shot roared, and the sizzling lead burned a hot path across Charity's left shoulder. She fired again and the turkey-necked outlaw folded in half, covering the Merwin and Hulbert revolver he held in his left hand.

"I need two men to help me take that body down to the constable's office," C. M. Rose announced. Quietly, inwardly, Charity Rose spoke to herself. "Two more to go."

Chapter 15

Burgeoning like the new summer, Charity's bank account increased steadily. For all her success, she was disturbed that she had seen no traces of either Horsley or Klinger. On the plus side, she had recently met Johnny Nolon, who owned the camp's largest gambling house. They found in each other a mutual challenge and a solid vein of respect. That respect, Charity found when she thought about it the past week, had begun to develop a romantic interest.

"He's a good-looking hunk of man," Timberline told her, as though reading her thoughts.

"Um-ah, who?"

"Don't play cute with me, honey. Johnny Nolon, of course. I can tell that look you've got in your eye. He's also lucky, whether he knows it yet or not."

"That's bald-faced flattery and you know it," Charity told her. "Do you have everything ready for our dinner tonight?"

Timberline made a face and stuck out her tongue. "See? Dinner in your suite, candlelight, an utterly sinful dress. I only hope it's mutual, honey."

Charity stood behind her desk. "Get out of here," she growled good-naturedly.

Sometimes of late, Johnny Nolon thought he might burst wide open. Especially since he met the dazzling redhead who had taken over the Old Homestead. Charity Carver was some woman. At his age, still on the youthful side of forty, he had believed that the lure of romance was safely out of the way. Cynical as only a gambler could be, he loved and left his women with no regrets. Why did he now have visions of vine-covered cottages with—oh, God!—kiddies running about? Russet-haired kiddies in these recent fantasies. They would dine together tonight, Johnny's thoughts went on. And then? For some reason his imaginings would not carry him into the realm of possible later delights. Humming lightly, Johnny put down his razor and wiped flecks of shaving lather from his face. He would dress and in fifteen minutes be on his way to the Old Homestead.

Closed for the Sabbath, the Old Homestead

provided a dignified, yet intimate background for the epicurean repast Charity laid on. Afterward they strolled under a moon in the first phase of waning from full. Frogs kept up an enormous bass while crickets and cicadas provided a buzzing string counterpoint. Fireflies winked in myriad number, their yellow-green phosphorous tails describing arabesques and chandelles in the cooling night air. After progressing to the edge of the treeline around the sprawling community of Cripple Creek, Johnny stopped under a huge old pine.

"I don't know when I've had such an enjoyable evening. We ought to make a practice of this. Only I insist that from now on I take you out for Sunday dinner."

"Johnny, I . . ."

"No, I won't hear it." He stopped suddenly and took her in his arms.

Charity responded instantly. Her own arms wrapped around his neck and their lips met with mutual accord. Although restrained, the kiss struck sparks of passion in each. Charity repressed a shiver of desire and left her cheek close to his when the embrace ended. An owl inquired what business they had disturbing his tranquility. Charity and Johnny laughed softly in response. Heady pine scent, one of nature's most abundant aphrodisiacs, generated urges deep within their beings.

"Johnny, there's a lot you don't know about me," she began uncertainly.

"And plenty you haven't learned about me,"

Johnny offered. "What else are Sunday night dinners good for except finding out? I know you have a prosperous business and a fantastic cook, er—ah, chef. But I want to take you out. To squire you around. We have our lives and there's no reason we shouldn't live them openly like others."

"Particularly those in comfortable circumstances?" Charity teased.

"People in glass houses, it's said," Johnny countered.

"Would you like to go back . . . for a nightcap and some talk?"

Johnny breathed deeply. "What's wrong with here? The pines make me drunk and moonlight softens even the harshest words."

"Who is considering harsh words?"

"Not I, sweet Charity. Nor you, I hope. Let's pledge that tonight is the first of many happy Sundays."

Charity affected a pout. "Must it be only Sundays?"

"I hoped you'd say that," Johnny responded eagerly. "Of course not. But this will be our . . . special day."

"Agreed. Shall we seal it with a kiss?"

Ardently they did.

Blissfully unaware of the pattern they established, Charity and Johnny spent the ensuing weeks anxiously anticipating their "special" Sunday nights. Their deep, abiding feelings for each other waxed warmly, lighthearted kisses giving way to gentle caresses. On a Sunday in late June, a summer thunderstorm kept them at the Old Homestead.

Soiled doves lounged about the lower rooms. Some played cards, others tatted or did crochet work, while a few, surprising to Johnny, read from a selection of classics Charity had installed in the small study off the central hall. She and her blooming love had sat down to a smoking brace of roast quail each when young Jason, the towel boy, came to the door with a message.

"Mr. Waterford is here, Miss Charity. He said to be sure and tell you he'd come without his blonde."

"Thank you, Jason." Charity smiled sweetly and patted his fine, straw-brown hair. To Johnny she turned another face. "Oh, damn. This had to happen now. I've got to see him. I have, ah, certain plans that are important to have him in the right frame of mind. I'll have the cook keep our supper hot. As a favor to me, Johnny, would you please take the back stair down for now and take your ease in the bar? As soon as I've dealt with Waterford, we can have the rest of the . . . ah, night to ourselves."

Johnny's eyebrows rose and he produced a crooked smile, which contrasted with the frown of annoyance that creased his brow. "So that's how it is, Miss Carver. You sweep one man out the back while you make ready to welcome a new suitor on the grand staircase."

Charity stuck out her tongue. "Oh pooh to

you. It really is business and it's terribly important. Half an hour?"

"I might be induced to wait that long. Any longer and some one of your charges will beguile me with their charms."

"You devil," Charity hissed, rushing to his arms and giving him a quick kiss.

Abner arrived five minutes later, in a huff from the delay. He lay his rain-wet note case to one side and accepted a glass of bourbon from Charity's hand. He greeted her stiffly and sat at the table which had so recently contained a romantic tablesetting for two.

"I'll come right to the point, Miss Charity. I am prepared to offer you full ownership of the Homestead."

Charity brightened and produced a pleased smile. "Oh, Abner, that's unquestionably generous of you."

"There are, ah, certain conditions." Abner prepared his first barb.

"Such as what?"

"First, that you, ah, submit to me for a period of one year."

"In everything, Abner?" Charity inquired warily.

"Exactly. 'Everything.' In spirit, in will, and in body."

"There are other conditions?" Charity pressed. Placed in the position of being of two minds, Charity congratulated herself on getting Waterford in the position where she wanted him. Part of her also felt a stab of fear that she had gotten into something she might not be able to handle.

"How far would such an agreement go?"

"Well, there will be a certain amount of pain involved for you," he began quite frankly. It chilled Charity to hear him speak so blandly about it. "But I promise I'll not scar your pretty face. I am, ah, afflicted with a certain unusual sort of need. To fulfill my desires, you'll be called upon to perform a number of, ah, unusual tasks."

Charity reached for the bell cord and rang, three short, crisp yanks. "That has . . . certain ramifications I would like to consider at length, Abner. Let's have a drink while I think it over."

"Delighted," Abner burbled. "Then, perhaps, we could begin the first, er, training session?"

"We'll see."

Timberline arrived and Charity ordered a pair of champagne cocktails. While she did, she placed the tip of her right little finger at the outer corner of her right eye and unobtrusively pulled downward. It was, Charity knew, the standard and accepted signal to give the indicated party a Micky Finn. Such a practice was followed in nearly every saloon and brothel in the nation. Timberline departed quickly, a mischievous smile quirking her lips. With Charity's dark and secret plan already in place to be instituted, tonight would be the night. Inwardly Charity rejoiced while she waited for the next stage to develop.

"Here are your drinks, Charity," Timberline announced five minutes later when she entered the room.

"Thank you, dear. Put them here on the table. Abner, to your good health."

"Ah, yes. And to yours," the millionaire responded.

They drank deeply and from a pitcher provided, replenished their glasses. Hardly two minutes went by before Abner's head began to nod. His chin sagged to his chest and he passed out with a gentle sigh. Charity took a deep breath and shook herself with relief as she again rang.

This time Timberline and Klugger both responded. "It's taken care of," she informed them. "Put Abner in Room Three-eleven. I'm planning to redecorate it and so it will be ideal. You know what to do after that?"

"Yes, Miss Charity," Klugger's rumbling bass sounded.

"Then I'll leave it all to your capable hands."

Charity left the private dining room and hurried down to the drawing room, where Johnny waited. The set of his shoulders and his expression betrayed a fretful jealousy over her being closeted with Abner. She eagerly crossed to him, arms open wide.

"Don't worry, my love. It's all over with now. I intend to feast you royally, then make love to you until your kingly brains fall out."

Pale light from a waning quarter moon streamed through the high, narrow window and fell across two figures on the large, canopied bed. Mirrors flanked the walls and duplicated the human forms, as did a special looking glass on the underside of the canopy. Light summer covers thrown back, legs entwined, Charity Rose and Johnny Nolon relaxed in the subsiding glow of recent, overpowering completion.

"You are one lovely woman," Johnny murmured softly, looking up at the reflected image of her body.

"You're quite a lot yourself, Johnny," Charity replied.

His compact, dark body, hardly three inches longer than her own, glowed a rich olive-amber in the Night Queen's rays. Here and there a pale pink line or puckered scar denoted the hazards of his chosen profession. The same, Charity had to admit, could be said for herself. In fact, she was surprised Johnny had not remarked over the bruise and burned stripe across her shoulder. Johnny's muscles seemed bunched and much too dense for the quick and limber moves required of a gambler.

"You know, I was seventeen before I ever made love with a woman," Johnny spoke in a near whisper.

"Really?" Charity found it amusing, and a bit sad. "How did that happen?"

"I'm not sure. The way I was raised, I suppose. I had two older sisters who had taken Holy Orders. My mother wanted me to enter the priesthood and my father wanted me to be a lawyer. My early years were about as sheltered as any person's could be."

"Poor, deprived little boy," Charity teased.

"I *was*. Until I discovered girls. Life was a misery for three long years, until I wound up in bed with the younger sister of my friend."

"Was it all you'd expected?" Charity asked, becoming aroused by the feel of his hard flesh against her own.

"Was it! All and more. That first time I thought I had died and gone to heaven. Half an hour later I knew for sure I hadn't. From what I'd been taught, they didn't do *that* up there, and I was glad I was still alive."

"Sometimes, the best things are worth waiting for," Charity advised.

"Was it like this? You and her alone and naked together, each of you using your hands on the other?" Charity asked in a low, husky voice as she began to stroke him.

"Y-yes. I was kinda scared, because she was three years younger. It turned out I needn't have been. She wound up taking the lead when I got scared."

"Did she get all wet inside like I am?"

"Oh, yeah, Charity. She surely did."

"And did she straddle you like this?" Charity asked as she spread her legs and settled athwart his hips, her hand never losing a stroke on his throbbing lance.

"Uh—uh-huh. Sh-she had to, 'cause I couldn't remember what to do," Johnny admitted.

Wildly aroused and enjoying the game, Charity continued eagerly. "Then did she take you in oh, so slowly, like this?" Charity asked her last question before she fully hilted him and began a wild and abandoned ride that sent shivers through her body and drew forth the deep well of experience Johnny had acquired since those long-ago days of youth. Once more they intensified their excitement by watching the mirrored canopy and walls.

"Hold me, Johnny," Charity whispered when they returned to normalcy. "Hold me close. There'll be more before morning, a whole lot more."

Chapter 16

Eventually the exhaustion of intense and frequent lovemaking overcame them. Charity and Johnny lay apart slightly, each soundly sleeping. At three-thirty in the morning there came an animal shriek from room 311. Charity bailed out of bed and into the filmiest, see-through wrap she owned. All the while, the masculine wails of horror continued.

"Wha—what's that?" Johnny demanded as he rubbed sleep out of his eyes while Charity ignited the gas jet.

"Oh, it's nothing. Just a little payback time," she dismissed lightly as the horrible wailing continued.

Before she left the room, Charity armed herself with one of her Bisleys. She ran into the hall where Klugger held Abner Waterford in a half nelson. The struggling millionaire was stark naked and continued to howl as Charity approached. Johnny Nolan had shrugged into trousers and appeared at the head of the stairs. From room 311 a disheveled old hag with white hair hobbled into the brighter light of the hallway. She had sores on her face and neck. Incongruous to this hideous apparition, she wore a fine silk nightgown.

Johnny recognized the disfigured woman as a local skid-row character from Poverty Gulch. Fireship Annie was reputed to be dying of every social disease known to man. Her toothless cackle sent a shiver along Johnny's spine. Abner Waterford suddenly went limp in Klugger's grasp and silenced his babbling.

"Well, Abner," Charity began in a brittle tone. "For once it appears that the punishment fits the crime. I retained Annie to see to it that the pox made you hobble to the grave and that the Spanish disease made certain you would enter there as a raving madman."

"Wu-wu-why? In the name of God, why?" Abner blubbered. His eyes had gone dull and his face slack at the awful knowledge of his fate.

Charity carefully omitted Louanne from her list of the avenged. "Because of what you did to Pearl, and what you intended doing to me, and for God only knows how many other poor women you either ruined, or drove to suicide, or tried to." She turned to the wretched slattern. "Annie, here's the hundred dollars I promised you for your, ah, special services. It's all right now. You can go home."

Muttering, Annie returned to the room to gather her clothing. Charity returned her attention to Abner. "Abner, I truly regret all of this. If you hadn't placed yourself so solidly above the law, none of this would have been necessary. I'm fully aware that society, as an institution, would never have punished you. I've learned the hard way that in many things, the giving or withholding of sex in particular, a woman has less rights than a dog. Had you curbed some of your excesses and not built so high a wall of protection about your person, there are many who would have applauded what you did. Now, though, you are going to suffer and continue to suffer until the moment you die."

Spit drooled from the corner of Abner's mouth. "You're the one who'll die, and soon, too. I'll have you killed for this. You can count on that."

"Anytime you want to try me," Charity goaded, holding the Bisley causally. "Throw him out, Klugger."

A week went by and the furor over the Independence bombing hardly abated. Entire blocks of shanties and shacks in Poverty Gulch and other miners' camps were thoroughly searched by militia troopers. The area had gotten too hot for Albert Horsley. He also considered an old score yet to be settled. Still in his guise as Harry

Orchard, and with a bulging money belt, he kissed his dutiful wife and step-kiddies on the porch of their cabin on Saturday morning.

"I'll be back, love, within a week," Harry promised. "Jamie, you take care of your mother, brother, and sister."

"Yes, sir," Jamie said brightly. "Hurry back. You ain't played baseball with us fellows for a long while. Maybe when you get home?"

"We'll see, son, we'll see."

At the depot, Harry got aboard the local to Denver where he would take the train for Boise, Idaho. It wouldn't do, he felt, to hang around these parts any longer.

"Do we have to have him around, Miss Charity?" Klugger complained. "Havin' that gunny of Johnny Nolan's around, following you, watchin' all the time, is bad for business."

"Johnny put him here because of Abner's threat," Charity replied lightly. "We don't really need him, but it makes Johnny feel that I'm safer. So we just put up with it."

When Johnny arrived half an hour later, Charity brought up the subject to him. She concluded with a light laugh. "I don't really need extra protection, Johnny. It's going to take another week before Abner knows for sure if he's infected. If he is, he'll be so busy trying to find a cure he won't have time to worry about me."

"Oh, sure. Is that why you bought that little

Merwin and Hulbert Pocket Army? Every lovely lady I know runs around with a short-barrel forty-four in her purse."

Charity frowned, caught in her own deception. "I learned my lesson with a number of different thirty-eights I've owned. The cartridge is too underpowered to be effective without a head shot or directly into the heart. Besides, I figure the Merwin will make an even better club than a Bisley."

Johnny gave her a peculiar look. "For a woman you certainly have an unhealthy knowledge of firearms and killing."

Charity forced a trill of laughter. "Johnny, Johnny, don't you remember our agreeing that there was a lot neither of us knew about the other? Let it lay and take me for a ride in the mountains. I'll die of boredom in this place."

He'd better let it be, Charity thought. If not, she'd have to find a whole new cover for hunting the badmen who flocked to the strife-battered district.

Bright and sunny, the next morning went unnoticed by Charity. Saturday night had been a big one. Some people, at least, had recovered from the pandemonium of the past weeks. They had money to spend and knew the right place to spread it around. The new superintendent, his managers and foremen from the Vindicator Mine, reserved the banquet hall for a huge dinner and entertainment. None of the Old Homestead staff got to sleep before three in the morning.

Sunday afternoon, Charity thought as she awakened at one o'clock. She stretched and thought of the fabulous hours she and Johnny had spent in her crisp, clean bed while the revelers roistered downstairs. Johnny had been more than usually attentive.

He had showered her nude body with kisses, lips and tongue working in concert to bring her total fulfillment.

"Now. Please now, Johnny." The words still echoed in memory. The images had their effect on her and Charity found her nipples hardening. Tired though she was, she became fully aroused. A bath, that would be the thing, she considered in an attempt to suppress her bubbling urges.

Bathed and dressed, though still feeling amorous, Charity came downstairs half an hour later. Johnny waited for her in the drawing room. He rose to his feet as she entered and took her hand.

"You look lovely," he murmured.

"Thank you, Johnny. I see you show no ill effects from last night."

"To the contrary, I have to walk bowlegged," Johnny quipped.

"Johnny! You're shameless. I suppose if it's so, we'll have to cancel our long afternoon, and dinner, and a rematch through tonight and tomorrow."

"Not so fast. I didn't say I was dead and ready to be buried."

"Well then, I might reconsider. Come on, I have to go over last night's receipts."

In the small office, Charity ran a finger down a column of figures and then counted the stacks of gold coins, flat sheaves of currency. These she placed in a large leather bag. A ringing of the bell summoned Klugger.

"Put this in the safe, Klugger. And, since I'll not be here in the morning, be sure it is deposited as soon as the bank opens tomorrow."

"Yes, Miss Charity," Klugger answered.

After he left the room, Charity made ready to depart. Johnny stood by the desk, hat in hand. The moment they were alone he began on a topic familiar to them both.

"I keep telling you that you're too trusting," Johnny chided gently. "What do you know about that brute? Or Timberline, for that matter. They could clean you out and be long gone before you suspected a thing. The way you do business around here is enough to give a person gray hair."

"Johnny, let's not talk about it today. Klugger is totally loyal to me because he is completely loyal to Timberline. He would no more conceive of stealing from me than he would of killing her. As for Timberline, from the first time I met her I know I could trust her. My father always told me I was an excellent judge of character and lately I've honed my ability. I never miss on judging someone, excepting, of course, an occasional lover."

"Oho! You're saying you don't trust me?" Johnny feigned hurt.

"Nothing of the kind."

They left the office and entered the bar. Johnny signaled to his hired gun, who came over, hat in hand. "Yes, sir, Mr. Nolon?"

"Nick, you can have the day off. Most of tomorrow, too. Report back here at six o'clock tomorrow evening. By then business will have started to pick up."

"Thank you, Mr. Nolan. I've been wantin' to spend some time with my woman and the kids."

Charity did a double take as the gun hawk departed. "He's married?"

"Not really. A woman from my place he's living with, ah, how is it? Without benefit of clergy. She has two youngsters who are tough as hell to handle. Nick sits down on them quite well. He and Lilly are satisfied with the arrangement, so they've never done anything official about it."

"I suppose that makes sense," Charity answered pensively. "Where are we going today?"

Johnny headed her toward the front door and the springy trap that waited outside. "Way up in the mountains, where there's nothing but trees and grass and bears. I'm sort of tired of people."

"Sounds wonderful," Charity admitted. "I haven't eaten, you know."

Johnny grinned. "All taken care of. There's sweet rolls and cheese on the seat and a picnic hamper in the back." He steered her to the small buggy and helped her aboard.

"Can we drive down through Poverty Gulch on the way?"

"I don't see why not," Johnny answered, snapping the reins.

As spindly wheels clattered on the sparsely graveled rut that described a road through Poverty Gulch, Charity looked about at the hovels occupied by the residents. "Isn't it a shame that human beings have to live like this? The two of us make so much money, we should do something about better housing conditions for these poor folks. Some of these shacks lean on each other. Remember what happened in the big fire? For safety's sake alone, we should try to help out."

Carefully picking his phrases, Johnny demurred. "Better housing costs bigger money. These people simply don't have it. The few who do are saving it to better themselves. I know, that's why you suggested we do something about it. If, through misdirected generosity, or pity, we forced better housing on them we'd either put them out on the street to beg, like Fireship Annie, or lock them into perpetual poverty by eliminating risk capital.

"Being a gambler, I know all about risk capital. Why, hell, it's better to let them risk some money at an honest game, like mine, than to take away all hope of self-betterment. And people want to do it for themselves. Giving them handouts, free housing, that sort of thing, breeds dependency. People dependent on others for everything, those without hope, become brigands and revolutionaries.

"It is a tenet of human nature that the status quo is never really satisfactory," Johnny went on, formulating his thoughts into clear, cogent words. "Risk is life itself. Any normal, healthy young person should find living on a predetermined, fixed income morally corrosive."

Charity swelled with pride at that. She'd never suspected Johnny of ever having a serious thought, let alone of being a philosopher.

Larks, wrens, and chickadees serenaded, their melodies punctuated by the frequent rat-a-tat-tat and cheeky scolding of woodpeckers. Squirrels hopped through the branches. Sunlight filtered by aspen leaves dappled the naked flesh of the couple tightly entwined on a mossy bank beside a stream. In slow, almost imperceptible movement, their bodies undulated in the throes of exquisite lovemaking.

"I've always preferred making love out of doors," Charity sighed as she felt Johnny thrust deeply within her. The languid nature of their blending created an agonizing excitement unlike any other.

"Maybe those university fellows are right

about our caveman ancestors," Johnny quipped as he felt her tighten around his rigid flesh.

"I don't know about that, but I had my first delightful experience outside by a pond, and it sort of shaped my outlook ever since," Charity responded.

Lying side by side, Charity asked Johnny about his plans for the evening. "Where are we going for dinner?"

"I made reservations at the National."

"The Brown Palace of Cripple Creek? How fancy," Charity laughingly replied.

"It's the best in town," Johnny defended. "Speaking of which, we had better get dressed and start back. It will be cool up here long before the sun sets."

"I'd like to go for a swim first," Charity suggested.

"That water would freeze you into a block of ice," Johnny informed her.

"Well then, I'll dab a bit and freshen up."

An hour later the trap rolled up the corner of Fourth and Bennett Avenue in Cripple Creek. The four-story, red-brick building, which was the National Hotel, glowed with gaslights. Rumor had it that the impressive structure had cost a hundred thousand dollars to build. At the top was the gabled penthouse of W. K. Gillett. Charity and Johnny dismounted and walked to the grand, glass-fronted entrance.

Inside, the lobby buzzed with chatter from the patrons waiting to be seated. Huge pots of ferns and tall vases of roses brightened the marble-floored expanse. The doors to the dining room stood open. Beyond could be seen a sea of white napery, with crystal candelabra on every table, along with silver bowls of bright summer flowers. Negro waiters in stiff-starched white jackets moved deftly among the diners, removing plates and filling glasses with champagne. Here and there one would set up a folding service and place a gigantic tray on it. He would lift metal lids from the savory food and serve a patron with flash and elegance. Johnny directed Charity to the captain who stood at the door.

"Table for Mr. Nolon," Johnny announced.

The captain checked his list. "Ah, yes. Here we are. Right this way, Mr. Nolon." He escorted them to a corner table, leaving behind the angry stares of those who had to wait their turn. He handed them menus; large gold-edged, red plush-covered folders that opened to snowy white pages and a truly elaborate list of dishes. "Your waiter will be with you momentarily. Enjoy your dinner."

Charity remarked several times that the food was superb. They lingered over a rich desert, then brandy for Johnny, a cordial for her and coffee. Blissfully unaware of it, they became nearly the last diners in the room. Charity had become witty and daring in her conversation and anticipated a particularly wonderful night of lovemaking. So did Johnny. After another half hour, the Maitre d' came to their table and called their attention to a couple who were departing. A quick glance around brought Johnny to the awareness that they were alone in the large hall.

Still laughing about it, Charity and Johnny stepped out into the street. They crossed the new concrete sidewalk to his sprightly trap. With a hand on her arm, Johnny helped Charity up into the buggy. Unexpected, Charity heard a loud, meaty smack behind her. Johnny's grip on her arm tightened as he lurched forward. A moment later, he stepped back, dragging Charity off balance. Charity fell forward, dropping her purse in the effort to catch herself and to brace them both.

Failing in that attempt, Charity fell under the spasming corpse of her lover. Burned into her memory was the horrifying impression of a yellow hickory axe handle protruding from Johnny's back.

"Klinger!" The name ripped from her throat.

Chapter 17

Knowledge of her impending death froze Charity for an instant. Her senses numbed and nothing made a clear impression for a long four seconds. Then a duck-quack babble turned into meaningful words.

"Ol' Bert's got you. You're gonna die, harlot. There's no way you can win outta this. The vengeance of the Lord is upon you."

With sound also came movement. Charity scrambled for her purse and the big .44-40 inside. A jolt of icy fear came when she failed to locate it. Part of her mind remained fixed on the awful sight of Johnny with the axe in his back. Another portion registered the clump-scrape approach of the club-footed madman.

"Wait'll I get my axe, then I'm gonna take your head clean off." Klinger's singsong came from close at hand.

Johnny's body lifted, then fell back as Klinger recovered his weapon. With the fascination of a bird for a deadly snake, Charity looked over her shoulder into Klinger's crazed eyes as his left hand grabbed Johnny's collar. As he started to fling the corpse aside, Charity made a sudden grab at the dead man's inside coat pocket, recalling the Smith Baby Russian he carried there.

Freeing the .38 revolver, Charity shot Klinger in the stomach. Startled, the crazed killer dropped Johnny's corpse across Charity's legs and hefted the dripping axe. Again Charity fired and a hole popped into the corded muscles of Klinger's chest. Rage ignited his bloodshot eyes. Wide of her mark, Charity's third bullet struck his neck and staggered the brute, who held the axe poised. It began to arc down as Charity hastily triggered the final two cartridges.

One slug took Klinger in the left eye, releasing a shower of dark fluid. The other broke his left wrist even as Charity twisted violently away. Sparks flashed in her peripheral vision as the axe head struck concrete, and Klinger fell across her dead lover. Belatedly, a horrified bystander came to her and helped free her from the weight of two dead men.

Chilled to the point of terror by the frightful incident, Charity stood trembling. She was further horrified to see a long hank of her auburn hair lying beside the axe scar on the pavement. Broken-hearted, Charity sank to her knees and lifted Johnny's body, cradling it in her arms.

"He's gone, miss. You'd best let go. There's nothing you can do," the bystander urged her uncertainly.

"No-no-no," Charity moaned. "It was my fault. He'd be alive if . . ."

Steadfastly she refused to release Johnny's corpse until she looked up into the disapproving face of Dr. Marcus McDade. How had he gotten here to Cripple Creek? Anger replaced the onset of grief in Charity's mind. If the whole world depended on it, Charity vowed, she'd be damned before she let that pompous, self-centered son of a bitch see her out of control. Gently she laid Johnny's head on the curb and came unsteadily to her feet.

When Charity regained the sidewalk, the bystander who had first aided her handed her the purse with the big Merwin and Hulbert inside. Glaring defiantly at Dr. McDade, she opened it and dropped the Smith and Wesson in beside her own gun. A wondering silence had descended on the small knot of people attracted by the gunshots. Shouldering them aside, Ed Cotter, the local beat patrolman, hurried to Charity's side.

"Ah, it's a terrible thing, it is," he said. "Poor Johnny. Any idea who that devil is that killed him?"

"His name is Klinger, Norbert Klinger," Charity answered, voice rusty with emotion. "He's wanted in Denver for escape and murder, also in three other places."

"There's little more we can do here," Ed told

her. "Will you please accompany me to the station and fill out a report?"

"Of course," Charity forced out. "Wh-what about Johnny?"

Cotter glanced back at the dead man. "He'll be taken care of, be sure of that. Johnny had lots of friends in Cripple Creek. By the way, who finished off his murderer?"

"I did," Charity said simply.

Johnny Nolon's funeral was a well-attended affair. The prosperous gambler, noted for the honesty of his dealers and gaming devices, had many friends. Of necessity Gen. Sherman Bell ordered an escort of militia troops to maintain order along the route to the cemetery. Bell's troops had continued the policy of rooting out union miners and hauling them in cattle cars across state lines to dump them without food, water, or means of protection on the wild prairies of Western Kansas and Nebraska, northern New Mexico, and southern Wyoming.

In instances where wives refused to be separated from their husbands, they and their children were given like treatment. A growing tide of protest to these tactics surfaced in the community. Some of Johnny's friends came to protest to Charity, stating the belief that men capable of such heartless cruelty should not be allowed to participate in Johnny's funeral. Too numb for outrage, Charity had nevertheless been aware of these travesties of justice since long before Johnny's death. Consumed by her grief, she could only respond bluntly with the truth.

"As I recall, you cheered those same troops on to exterminate every single union miner in the district following the Independence bomb disaster. What makes that laudable behavior so terrible now?"

They soon stopped coming to her with their complaints. Regardless of Charity's position, Timberline remained indignant as hell over what was happening. She even insisted upon taking in some of the homeless and penniless miners' families. Indifferent in her grief, Charity allowed it without comment. The upper stories of the Old Homestead soon bulged with children and women, too grateful for a place to stay to complain about the nature of business conducted there.

Not that business remained all that brisk. After Johnny's death, Charity lost the patronage of many of the district's wealthier citizens. In spite of her melancholy mood, she soon realized this. Johnny had not only been close to her heart, he held the key to her success at the Old Homestead. This left her pulled in two directions.

On one hand vengeance had come too swiftly. She would like to see Norbert Klinger's corpse torn apart by crows. But society would hardly condone that. On the other, she had to do something about the future of her establishment.

Someone else had been aware of Charity's situation. Abner Waterford observed from a distance and brooded over the unspeakable deceit she had pulled on him. He bided his time until a full week after Johnny Nolon's funeral. Then he decided the time was right to exact payment for her transgression. He had three reasons that suggested this.

First, Charity had lost the sponsorship of one of the wealthier citizens of the district with the death of the gambling kingpin. And with it the patronage of many more. Secondly, with so much violence and disruption, considering that Charity was harboring the wives and children of some union miners, one more incident would receive little attention. Lastly, he had begun to drip. And burn, and itch, and sting. Not even the infidelities and eventual betrayal by his former wife had given him such intense physical pain. He firmly believed that any day the sores would begin to appear. And for that, Charity must die.

"We keep it simple," Abner explained to the two men he had chosen to aid him. "Only the three of us will know about it. The house is closed on Sunday and doesn't open until four, Monday afternoon. We'll go in at two in the morning, Monday. That will give us close to four hours before daylight. Everyone should be in bed asleep. Remember, our only target is Charity. If anyone gets in the way, however, they'll have to die."

Silent as ghosts, Abner's two henchmen drifted

up to the side of the Old Homestead. From a distance came the notes of a piano. Here and there a lantern glowed yellow in a window, where sickness or an inability to sleep kept residents about in the night. A few dogs barked at shadows or a straying skunk. The redolent odor of the latter floated in the air around the raiders.

"Phew! D'you smell that, Homer?" Lem Carter whispered.

"How could I help but smell it, Lem? Where's Waterford?"

"Right behind you, Homer," Abner Waterford spoke out of the shadows. "If you had half a brain you'd have found me by now."

"How do we get in here without making noise?" Lem, the somewhat more intelligent of the pair, asked.

Abner moved closer to them to reduce the possibility of being overheard. "Charity is entirely unaware that I have a key to the coal chute door. We're going to slide down into the cellar and work our way up from there."

"Ummm. I don't know about that," Homer complained. "Fallin' scares me."

"Now's a fine time . . ." Abner started. "Close your eyes and you'll never know it happened."

The trio's ride to the coal pile went unnoticed by the Old Homestead's slumbering residents. Remarkably no one received more than a scraped palm when Abner and his companions made contact with the rough-edged fuel below. Lighting a candle he brought along for the purpose, Abner led the way to the steep stairs that would take them to the first floor.

Undetected, they entered the large kitchen of the establishment. Abner drew Lem and Homer close. "First make sure that Klugger is not prowling around. Then we start upstairs." A thin smile of anticipation stretched Abner's lips.

Lem and Homer spread out. Each took a side of the lower floor, divided by the hallway. Eyes straining against the darkness, Homer turned into the drawing room. Dozing lightly in a padded wing chair sat Klugger. His big arms dwarfed the eight-gauge shotgun he held. The rhythm of his slumber fluttered his lips with each exhalation. Caught unprepared, Homer could think only of how quickly a single, well-placed shot would end it.

Strident clicks from Homer's cocking hammer instantly awakened Klugger. His shotgun boomed loudly in the confines of the room. Buckshot whistled through the air and rattled as it punched holes in the plaster. Homer had dropped instantly when he saw his proposed victim stir. He rolled to one side and returned fire.

Klugger grunted softly and triggered the other barrel. Three shots burned painful trails down Homer's back. The rest of the shot column went high. Homer fired again and missed. Klugger stood and broke open the shotgun. Quickly he extracted the spent casings and slid two fresh brass tubes into place. He closed the breech in a deliberate manner and took careful aim at Homer.

From the doorway, Abner Waterford fired at the

same time as the determined bouncer. A split second later he triggered a second round. Both slugs blasted their way into Klugger's chest. His heart exploded even as he tilted the muzzles of his scattergun toward the ceiling and let off one barrel. He sank to his knees before toppling sideways into death.

"Damn. Sure glad you were there," Homer gulped out.

Shouts of alarm came from the second floor. "No need to whisper now. Looks like everyone knows we're here," Abner complained.

"We better get upstairs then," Lem advised.

Homer winced as he moved and put a hand on his back. "Damn, got me a few scrapes from buckshot. Stings like all get out."

"Worry about it later, Homer. We got to make sure Charity doesn't slip away."

Impatient now that they had lost the element of surprise, Abner Waterford led the way. In the second floor hall, frightened children ran about crying and shrieking, while women obviously not soiled doves called out to them and to God for deliverance. A small derringer popped twice and bullets gouged the wallpaper close to Lem's head. Ignoring the now empty weapon, he grabbed the young whore roughly and yanked her close.

"Your boss? Where's Charity?" he growled.

"I . . . I don't know," she peeped in a tiny voice.

"Don't lie to me, sister," Lem threatened.

"I'm not. She's . . . acted sort of funny since Johnny got killed. Never know if she's here or not."

Lem thrust her away from him and started for the stairway to the top floor. Homer and Abner had preceded him. Cries of fright and a steady howl of pain reached Lem's ears. Abner had a soiled dove against the wall, one big, meaty hand slapping her face over and over. Spittle flew from the enraged man's lips as he shouted at her.

"Where is she? Where's Charity. Answer me!"

Preceding his henchmen, Abner started for the stairway which led upward to the private suite where he expected to find Charity. He had her now. There would be no escape from the vengeance he would extract. With each step his expectation grew.

"She'll rue the day that sick idea occurred to her," he whispered to himself.

Utter darkness in the stairwell slowed Abner. He groped along the wall, defining its dimensions with sensitive fingers. One boot toe rapped on a riser. He daren't use his candle, he reminded himself as he cursed the darkness, which also provided them their only protection. Tingling with the tension of the invasion, Abner reckoned he was halfway there.

Compelled by his anxiety to successfully end it, Abner charged the rest of the way in a rush. A pandemonium of women's voices surrounded him. Darkness turned suddenly to intense light as gas lamps blazed in the second floor hallway around

Abner. Dimly, his mind racing, he heard behind him the clump of boots in the hall. He caught at a screaming prostitute who ran past him and slammed her against the wall.

"Where is she?" he demanded. "Where is Charity?"

"She's not here," the frightened young woman responded.

"You're lying." Enraged, Abner began to backhand her. The sound of his men's footsteps grew closer.

"Where is she? Where's Charity? Answer me!"

"I'm right behind you, Abner," the husky voice declared.

Muffled, but distinct enough to register, the report of a shotgun awakened Charity Rose from a fitful sleep. She came upright, threw back the covers and swung her legs out of bed to the accompaniment of more gunfire. She tugged on a heavy wrap and filled her right hand with the stallion's neck grip of a Bisley. She cocked the weapon as she crossed the floor. Shrill shouts and cries for mercy came from beyond.

It could be anything from the militia rounding up unionist wives in a new wave of terror, to Abner Waterford actually carrying out his threats of revenge. No matter how it worked out, Charity had no intention of meekly submitting. She opened the door to see the familiar figure of Abner Waterford, hunched over a terrified hooker. Ignoring all else, Charity hurried in their direction. As she approached, she heard Abner's demands.

"I'm right behind you, Abner," she barked in a husky tone.

Stung by the sound of her voice, Abner Waterford made another terrible mistake in his life. His right hand snatched for the fancy, nickle-plated Smith and Wesson in his shoulder holster as he turned toward his enemy.

"You're dead, bit—" Abner's words cut off at sight of the steady muzzle of the Colt Bisley in her hand.

He couldn't so quickly stop the movement of his hand. His Smith five-shot revolver flashed brightly in the gaslight a fraction of a second before Charity shot him in the chest. Reflex slammed Abner around and backward. His Smith barked sharply, and the young prostitute yelped in pain at the gouge the bullet put in her shoulder. Abner went over balance and flopped gracelessly to the floor. In a flash he was scrambling into the darkness on hands and knees. Charity quickly recognized Abner's henchmen and put a bullet in Lem's right thigh, then went after Abner.

Cautiously she entered the stairwell. No sign of Abner. A trail of blood led down the risers toward the second floor. With a bounding stride, she took the steps two at a time. Charity followed the crimson trail to the room Timberline used. Abandoning prudence, she flung the door open and dived into the room. Abner's gun barked once, missing Charity, then Timberline was at him, clawing and biting. Abner turned the small revolver and fired again.

With a cry of agony, Timberline fell away. Charity's Bisley spoke with finality, and a big, black .45 hole appeared in Abner's forehead. His head snapped back and he swayed like a mighty tree. The Smith slipped from his hand and he flopped full length on Timberline's bed. Boot toes rapped a final tattoo on the wooden floor.

"Oh, God, he shot you," Charity blurted as she came to her feet and rushed to the side of the bed.

"I—I feel all hollow inside. Is it bad?" Timberline asked in a small, unnatural, little-girl voice.

With fumbling fingers, Charity examined the wound. Red-purple intestine strained to escape the entry wound, as though endowed with separate life. Gently the bounty hunter reached around and felt the jagged skin around a slightly larger exit wound. Blood flowed freely, but thankfully the bullet had not hit bone and expanded.

"I, ah, think you'll live," Charity said dry-throated. "The holes aren't too big."

"What do we do with these two?" a large, no-nonsense miner's wife asked from the doorway.

Charity looked to see Lem and Homer thoroughly cowed by a variety of firearms, including an ancient Colt's Dragoon pistol. "Hold them downstairs and send someone for the sheriff. One of you get me some clean water and something to make bandages, and send for a doctor. Timberline . . . Timberline's been hurt."

Doctor Kramer had come, treated Timberline, with the warning that the worst might not be over, and gone by the time Sheriff Bell at last arrived. He stormed in and took custody of Lem and Homer, who bleated out that the crazed woman who ran the place had killed Abner Waterford. The sheriff confronted Charity in her suite.

"Are you prepared to surrender peacefully?" he demanded when he entered.

"What for, sheriff?" Charity asked mildly.

"For the murder of one of our leading citizens, Abner Waterford, what else, woman?"

"Just a minute, sheriff. Let me tell you a little something about this leading citizen." For the next ten minutes, Charity unraveled the sordid tale of Abner Waterford's secret life. At her conclusion the sheriff remained thoughtfully silent.

"If you're inclined to a possible solution, sheriff, I would suggest that it would be much better if word went out that Abner committed suicide in a fit of drunken despondency. Perhaps he'd been brooding over the unfairness of his former wife?"

"Yet the fact remains you killed him," the lawman stubbornly insisted.

"He was armed at the time," Charity reminded him. "He seriously wounded my business associate and killed my house manager, Mr. Klugger. I hardly think that makes him an 'innocent victim.'"

"Humph, ah, yes. I get your point. Still this is going to be hard to explain."

"Why, sheriff. Surely you can be inventive. I happen to know that Abner's will leaves everything to charities of his choice, as well as all the foundations he has already established. His behavior, if the details were known—as they surely would were I to go to trial for his killing—would cast doubt on his sanity, and his deservedly disinherited relatives would seek to break the will. An onus would even hang over the new orphanage in Denver."

"That, ah . . . sounds likely enough," Sheriff Bell wavered.

"No jury of western men would convict me for what I've done. Particularly since Timberline, the mortician, and even Abner's latest victim, would testify to the truth."

"In that case, I think it prudent if we deport those variety show bad men Abner had with him just like they were union miners."

"Thank you, sheriff. It's nice to see the law working in favor of the little man," Charity managed with only the slightest hint of sarcasm.

Downstairs, the sheriff confronted Lem and Homer, who quickly saw the wisdom of departing without comment. "We'll be willing to swear an oath of secrecy, sheriff, provided you forget we were ever present," Lem offered.

"Right, sheriff. We ain't stupid, ya know," Homer added.

Sheriff Bell shrugged. "What the hell? Who'd believe a pair of barroom boasters anyway. Though better you do your boasting, if any, in

Kansas."

At the depot, he had them registered as union sympathizers and slated for departure on the next train east. By noon normalcy had returned to the Old Homestead, and Sheriff Bell reported his actions to Charity.

"You've been most understanding and helpful, sheriff. I don't mean to be trite, but I hope that with this, we can let sleeping dogs lie."

Chapter 18

Demons born of inflamation of her wounds, yet all the same real, tormented Timberline. She thrashed on her bed and moaned, slipping in and out of consciousness. Charity Rose felt obliged to stay at her side and nurse the courageous young woman back to health. She had little else to do, Charity consoled herself. The verve had gone out of the mining district.

Cripple Creek and the camps were dividing themselves into ethnic neighborhoods. Saloons in the center of town, once the most prevalent business, were folding. Constant monitoring of the house receipts indicated that there had been a sharp drop in business; particularly the most lucrative in regard to the house, that of food and beverage. Likewise, Charity soon found the best girls leaving for new boomtowns to the north and west, in Idaho, Nevada, and Montana.

Worse, from Charity's point of view, the supply of wanted men seemed to have dried up with the coming of martial law and a reorganization of local law enforcement. The contributions of C. M. Rose to Charity's bank balance reached a point of next to nothing. Through all of this, she fretted over her friend's condition, blaming herself in part for the nearly fatal wound.

"Somehow," Charity told the delirious, suffering Timberline, "somehow we'll find a way to come out ahead in the end."

"I say you're sucked right up to the asshole of these damned unionists," Sam Steele snarled, his slate-gray eyes hard and fixed on the rather mild-looking man at the bar.

"Look, Mr. Steele, I don't have any argument with you. I've never taken sides with the union."

Silence hung in the old Ford Exchange, now called Mantleys. Several patrons had cleared away from the mahogany, leaving a vast expanse of bar and brass rail between Sam Steele and the man he had suddenly picked on. No one who had been in Cripple Creek for long dared to move or otherwise distract the deadly gunman. The victim of Steele's verbal attack swallowed hard and tugged at a too-tight collar.

"I say you're a goddamned liar. Your father was a liar and a coward and your mother was a whore. Your sister—"

Steele's goading was enough. The young mining

surveyor went for his six-gun in spite of his knowledge of Sam Steele's prowess with firearms. Steele was that extreme rarity, a deadly hipshot and utterly cold and unflappable. His simulated anger had no bearing on the calculating murderer behind the deputy's badge.

Even going off the other's move, Steele had his Colt clear of leather and the hammer falling before the youthful surveyor touched the butt of his revolver. The blast hurt ears all round the bar. Steele's safety shot, although completely unnecessary, blew off the back of the unfortunate young man's head. Steele felt a ripple of satisfaction.

He had killed for very little reason, he admitted to himself, mostly to keep the town afraid of him. He had felt his power slipping of late and this would keep them on their toes for a while longer.

Hat in hand, Spec Penrose stood on the verandah of the Old Homestead. Beside him, Charity Rose looked askance at the real estate broker, while ostensibly examining the flowers that had opened their faces in window boxes.

"I'd be most honored if you'd agree to go to the National with me for dinner tomorrow night, Miss Charity. I know that a proper mourning period has not been observed, but it's not good for you to stay cooped up here all the time. This is not a romantic invitation, only a friend offering his modest company to help you regain your spirits."

"Ummmm. Well, in that case, perhaps . . . yes. I'll be delighted to go to dinner with you, Spec.

What time will you call for me?"

"Is seven o'clock too early?"

"Not at all. I'll be expecting you."

"Thank you, Miss Charity. Good day."

With Spec walking down the path to the street, Charity reflected that he had been paying a bit more attention to her of late. Could that be because of the terms of the partnership in the Homestead left the entire establishment to the surviving partner? Perhaps that was unkind. Spec had rocketed up to become one of the bigger tycoons of the district, primarily through sale and resale of the same properties as the fortunes of the mining communities waxed and waned. So one could consider him well-to-do. In that light, Charity didn't know whether to feel flattered or suspicious. Wealth breads power, her father used to say. And power breeds the lust for more power. Perhaps he was after the Homestead after all.

Actually she didn't care. Timberline had taken a strong, positive turn toward recovery and Charity felt like celebrating. She had planned a day of shopping, browsing through the shops in the heart of town and arranging for some much needed commoditites for the Homestead. Spec's unannounced visit had delayed her. Adjusting the drape of the shawl over her shoulders, she stepped off the porch and started on her rounds.

Nothing submerged a woman's anxieties like a therapeutic spree in the nearest stores. Charity reveled in it, trying on clothes, examining fabric for new curtains on the second floor, ordering rare and exotic foods for the kitchen of the Homestead. She stepped out of the wine merchant's establishment and glanced along the block to the post office, only to see a familiar and chilling face. Albert Horsley!

Before she could react, Horsley turned from the door to the post office and disappeared into a crowd of loafers lounging at the mouth of an alley. Charity hurried to the small building that housed the U. S. Mail. She entered and perfunctorily greeted Mrs. Clara Rogers, the postmistress.

"Clara, do you know that man who just came out of here?"

"Of course I do. He's Mr. Harry Orchard." In glowing words of praise she spent five minutes extolling the virtues of the wonderful Mr. Harry Orchard. The more Clara spoke, the more Charity came alive again. Armed with her new knowledge she went directly to the livery stable where she switched to the persona of C. M. Rose. From there she called on the sheriff's office.

"I have here a wanted poster for one Albert O. Horsley, from Idaho, and I have specific information that Horsley is in Cripple Creek. I want a warrant for his arrest, and I'd appreciate it if you, sheriff, came along with me to assist in his capture."

"Whoa there, little feller. How does it come you're so suddenly sure of yourself? You've brought in some mean customers, but this Horsley is a madman, a bomb expert who's killed a whole lot of people."

"Including the super and foreman at the Victor and the miners in Independence, I'm willing to bet," Charity told him.

"In that case, you ought to go to the militia," Sheriff Bell opined.

"I came here because I thought you might like to regain your standing with the people of Cripple Creek. Besides I don't entirely trust Gen. Bell."

"Humph. He is, after all, my brother." At Charity's icy stare, he continued hesitantly. "Well then, I suppose we can do it. Judge Morris should be in his office about now. We'll call on him and set out. Where are we going, by the way?"

Charity nodded to the far end of town. "Not far. Only to Poverty Gulch."

"Steee-rike three!" Harry Orchard bellowed, bent over the catcher in his position as umpire. "That finishes it, fellows."

A chorus of yells, groans, and complaints answered him. Harry pulled off his thin chest pad as several boys crowded around him. He patted one freckled redhead on his sunburned scalp.

"You did a great job today, Luke. Keep that up and you'll be getting paid to play baseball."

"Awh, Harry," the shy youngster replied, eyes lowered, one worn shoe toe scuffing the ground.

"I mean it. Say, that cardboard box over there has some horehound sticks and licorice whips for everyone. Go help yourselves."

With the throng rapidly departed, Harry set off for home. His thoughts drifted. He'd not accomplished anything by his short trip to Idaho. He would, he knew, try again. Meanwhile, outside of busting his ass for an honest living, he had no prospects in Cripple Creek. The Western Federation of Miners was a thing of the past. Not one unionist remained in the various camps. Certainly none with the desire or the funds to hire his talents. He had another plan, though; one he had worked at off and on.

One of the boys whose confidence he had won was Bobby Tutt, son of Spec Penrose's partner in the prosperous real estate firm. Little Bobby was fascinated about anything involving baseball. He was a skilled player, though somewhat younger than most of the other boys. The bright-eyed ten-year-old had even stayed over at the Orchard home, with Harry's stepson, when the team was taking an early local to Creede to play another scratched-together nine. From that very date, Harry contemplated how easy it would be to kidnap little Bobby and hold him for a truly fabulous ransom. Where he would hold him was easy.

Several of the mines had run into subterranean water, and miles-long drifts had been run to drain them. Harry figured he could hold the boy in one of these. He'd even built a cell-like room in one where a ventilator shaft made a wide juncture. Harry stocked it with canned food and a hose, through which his prisoner could draw water from the drainage ditch. The real problem, one which had delayed his plans so far, was in how to figure out a means to exchange the boy, or his location, for the cash, without getting caught — or more likely, shot. Harry still puzzled over it when he came in sight of his cabin. What he saw stopped him so abruptly he staggered forward a couple of steps.

There was his wife, with Sheriff Bell and that goddamned gunslick bounty hunter, C. M. Rose. Not only was she talking to them right polite and all, she was holding wide the door and welcoming them inside. Harry could think of only one reason for that. Without further hesitation, he took off across country toward the refuge of the cell that he had prepared for Bobby Tutt.

Mildred Orchard poured more tea. "I can't understand why he hasn't returned. He's usually finished by now."

"Work?" Charity inquired politely in the guise of C. M. Rose.

"Oh, no, Harry's been laid off for some time, Mr. Rose. He's playing baseball with the younger boys this afternoon. My, he's so regular in his habits I don't know what could have delayed him."

"The, ah, ball diamond," Sheriff Bell said quietly. He and Charity exchanged glances.

"If I knew what your business was with Harry I'm sure I could convey it to him when he does come."

Charity decided to take the risk. "Mrs. Orchard, your husband's name is not Orchard. It's Albert O. Horsley. He is wanted for murder in Idaho, involving the bombing of a mine. Also he has a wife and children there, whom he abandoned when he came here for the union. We believe that he is responsible for the Vindicator explosion and the Independance Station massacre also."

Mildred turned white. She dropped her second best teapot and it shattered at her feet. Her tremors could soon be identified not with shock and hurt, but with fury. "No!" she shouted. "No, that's not true. You're lying. Get out of here, get out! Harry's a good man. I'll not listen to this. Get out!"

Somewhat sheepishly, Charity and Sheriff Bell did.

Five days in a black hole had given Harry Orchard an overwhelming dose of cabin fever. He wanted to slam his fists against the walls and scream. During his enforced hibernation, he let his imagination have free reign. He could, he was now certain, trace all his troubles back to Governor Steunenberg of Idaho. It was he who put the pesky reward on Harry. If it hadn't been for that, that double-damned C. M. Rose would never have come looking for him. After the fifth day of brooding over this unforgivable injustice, Harry decided to do something about it. He needed to leave this pest hole anyway.

His last candle guttered in a pool of melted wax. His watch had stopped and he was down to two cans of beans. Time to move on and rectify some of the wrongs done him. He made a careful check of the shaft, making sure it was dark outside, then gathered his bomb-making gear into a backpack with the last of the beans and some stale bread. He formed his blankets into a horseshoe around the pack and tied them securely. Then he loaded pellets of carbide into his lamp and charged it with water. Lighting it with the remains of the candle, to save the flint, he slipped into the packstraps, settled the load on his shoulders and started out.

Chapter 19

Two dozen roosters, a bag-full milk cow, and Charity Rose greeted the early, pastel dawn. Trudging back to the Old Homestead before the citizens of Cripple Creek got up and about, Charity shed her guise as C. M. Rose and dressed in a particularly flattering frock. Then she prepared a tray with coffee, rolls, and butter and took it to Timberline's room. After the preliminaries, Charity confided in her friend.

"I god dis code in my heb," she said in discomfort. Translated by a sympathetic Timberline, the rest went this way. "I've sat out for four nights now, keeping watch over the Orchard house. No sign of Harry. I've been nursing this miserable cold for two days. All I've gotten out of it is worse."

"Awh, honey, that's terrible. Look; what you need is some of that Mexican cactus juice, lemon, and honey. I'm feeling a lot more fit than before I got shot. Let me go out and find what will fix you right up. A day in bed, lots of tequila and lemon with honey and you'll bounce right back."

"Oh, Timber, I can't let you d—"

"You nursed me all through the awful times, so no way I'll let you go without some good old-fashioned care."

No protest Charity could think of could deter her. Timberline dressed with more enthusiasm than Charity had seen in weeks. She collected her comb, coin purse, and other items and secured them in her clutch purse, then donned a wide-brimmed hat and sallied forth. Charity wished her a plugged-nose good luck.

Half a block from the Old Homestead a woman strange to Timberline stopped her on the street. "Excuse me. I noticed you came from the, ah, that place. I'm Mrs. Harry Orchard. Might I prevail upon you to convey my apologies to Mr. C. M. Rose, whom I understand lives at the Homestead?"

"I, ah, wu—well, yes. I'll do that. Any other messages?" an off-balance Timberline responded.

"N-no. Nothing at this time, anyway."

When Timberline returned, she had the cook prepare a steaming hot cup of tequila, lemon juice, honey, and water. This the titanic tart urged on her friend, while she withheld reporting the incident until Charity consumed half the contents of the large ceramic mug. The story at last told, Charity nodded understandingly.

"That means only one thing. The woman has seen her husband . . . and not believed him. I can still score this one for the home team." Charity paused a moment. "Harry Orchard might like that one."

"You're not going out again, not in your present condition," Timberline protested.

"I've got to. Cold or no, C. M. Rose rides again," Charity expounded.

"Oh, no," Timberline groaned. "At least it's a hot, sunny day out there."

Rigged in her garb, Charity revisited the Orchard cabin. Mildred eagerly confided in her. "It was just at daybreak. I awoke to a scratching on my window. It was Harry. He wanted money and his rifle."

"What rifle was that, Miz Orchard?" C. M. Rose asked.

"Ah, I believe it was a Seventy-six model Winchester."

"Was it an Express rifle?"

"I . . . I believe it was. A forty—forty-something."

"Forty-sixty-five?" Charity suggested, recalling the long-range sniping deaths.

"Yes, that's it. I confronted Harry with what you had told me. He denied everything," Mildred continued. "But I could tell he was lying. I know now that he is a mass murderer and a bigamist. I'm so ashamed. But I pretended to support him, lest the children and I be added to his list of victims. I saw him off and wished him well."

"Do you know where he's going?"

"He said something about having to return to Idaho again."

"Thank you, Miz Orchard. Can you tell me why you sent a message to me, instead of taking it to Sheriff Bell?"

Assuming a new dignity, Mildred answered straightforwardly. "I'm the widow of a union miner, murdered by that monster Sam Steele. I could never bring myself to deal with the sheriff, who supports that sort of man."

"You could have come to me yourself and had assured privacy."

"As a wife and mother, and a good Christian, I could hardly be expected to enter the Old Homestead. I'd been watching that, ah, place since early morning to find someone I dare approach. The tall girl, the one folks call Timberline, came out and I asked her to tell you."

"You've been quite brave, Miz Orchard. Thank you so much."

Tears appeared in Mildred's eyes. "If—if Harry's already married to someone else, then I'm not really his wife. We've been living in sin. Oh, what will the children think?"

"Nothing if you don't tell them. I'm certainly not going to let anyone know."

"Oh, bless you, sir." Mildred paused and a

question formed. "What are you going to do, then?"

"Go get a warrant and head for Idaho," Charity told her simply.

"That man is a menace to the whole country," Sheriff Bell said of Albert Horsley. "If you want a badge, you've got it. And we'll have that warrant in no time."

"Thank you, sheriff," C. M. Rose replied.

Sheriff Bell dug through his desk and came up with a deputy's badge. He handed it to Charity and started to administer the oath when the door opened and five highly agitated people entered. Led by Cynthia Gleason, the members of the Citizen's Alliance had mustered courage enough to approach the sheriff with their paramount problem.

"Sheriff." Cynthia Gleason took the lead. "You have to do something about the lawlessness of those hired guns led by Sam Steele."

Sheriff Bell winced. "What is it you propose I do?"

"Why, fire them, of course," Cynthia Gleason responded.

With the state militia departed and Steele riding high and mighty over the town, Sheriff Bell hesitated to force a confrontation. Particularly when he knew that for all their protests, not a one of these good citizens would back him against the notorious gunfighter. He tried again to stave off the inevitable.

"Well, now, it's not as easy as all that. I can't simply go out and say, 'Sam, you and your gunnies are fired.' You must consider what could happen if he didn't listen to me."

"Bu-but you're the law," the determined woman spluttered. "It's your job to—to..." Recognizing the defeated expression on the sheriff's face, Cynthia turned elsewhere for assistance. "What's the going rate for a killing?" she asked of C. M. Rose.

"Well, now, I'm sure I wouldn't know," Charity said. "I'm not a hired gun, ma'am. I'm a bounty hunter. Get a price put on Steele's head and I'll go after him."

Charity's words prompted the sheriff to consider another possibility. "What would you charge to back me up, provided I could get Steele into the office by himself?"

A brief smile flickered on Charity's lips. "Now, I reckon that to be a citizen's simple duty. No charge, sheriff."

Bell turned a triumphant smile on the Citizen's Alliance. "There you have it, folks. It might take us a little while, but I think I can assure you now that Mr. Steele will no longer menace you after today. All I ask is that you try not to look too smug and satisfied when you leave here."

Cynthia Gleason became effusive. "Oh, bless

you, Mr. Rose. And thank you, sheriff. I think we can think of a few nasty things to say on the way out so that any of Steele's spies will not be any the wiser."

After the delegation departed, Sheriff Bell stuck his head out the door and called to an urchin lounging at the tie rail. "Petey!" When the boy approached, the sheriff flipped him a five cent piece. "Go find Mr. Steele and ask him to come to the office at his convenience."

Eyes opening wide at the importance of his mission, the lad caught the coin and started off. "Yes, sir, sheriff."

Back inside, Bell explained his play to Charity. "The Alliance has relayed complaints through me several times. If Steele knows of their visit today, he'll assume their efforts got similar results as before. He's contemptuous enough of me, I'm shamed to admit, that he'll not bring a bodyguard along in any event. Once we get him in here, with you backing my play, we can demand he turn in his badge. Without that authority to prop him up, I'm sure his gang of gunhawks will desert him. So now all we have to do is sit and wait."

Sam Steele was indulging in a pre-lunch drink in the back room of the Nugget Exchange. The mop-haired urchin, Petey, found him there and delivered the message. He also passed on the information that some of the snooty folks from the Citizen's Alliance had been to see the sheriff and had left with mighty dark looks. Steele laughed, toussled the boy's hair and gave him a silver dollar. The gunfighter finished his whiskey and started off for the sheriff's office.

He entered filled with self-importance and confident of absolute power. "So they came around whining again, eh? I trust you sent them packing."

"Well, they weren't pleased," Bell hedged. "I'm sure you can understand that their concerns are not of a trivial nature. That is, I . . ." He glanced at C. M. Rose and cleared his throat. "I, ah, have to ask you for your badge. Sam, that last killing was inexcusable. It has left me with no other course. I, ah, must have that badge and I expect you to be clear of town by this evening."

Surprise raised Sam Steele's eyebrows. He, too, glanced at Rose. Then he shrugged and reached for the badge with his left hand. "Too bad y'all had a fallin' out."

His ruse almost worked. It must have been the slight hitch of his right shoulder that launched Charity into action as she rocked back, her thumb raking the Bisley hammer to full cock. Even as she did, her fingers pulled the Colt backward from the leather and tripped the trigger.

Steele had cocked his weapon and held it

level, with his elbow extended to lock-on—which gave him his deadly accuracy—with the center of Charity's chest. Her 250 grain slug took him in the hip joint. The jar of impact reached Steele's gun hand in time to ruin his aim. He placed his slug through a fold of cloth in Charity's shirt at waist level. Gun forward now, in a two-hand grip, Charity rotated the hammer back when she sensed the numbers running out.

With a shift of weight, she delivered a kick to Steele's left hip that dropped him and spoiled his second shot. Sheriff Bell finally entered the play, more than a fraction late. His bullet shattered the window at the level where Steele's head had been. Fortune had reversed itself. Now Sam Steele sat on the floor and belatedly dragged his hammer back when the Bisley's sights framed his head.

Small, even teeth biting the inside of her lower lip, Charity stroked the trigger. Flame erupted from the muzzle and she saw Steele's head jerk through the halo of smoke.

"Jeezus! Smack through the runnin' lights," Sheriff Bell blurted in awe.

The rush of combat deserted Charity and she sagged against the desk. It had happened so quickly she had even time to think, to plan her actions. Sucking in a great draught of smoke-tinged air, Charity spoke somewhat shakily.

"If you'll check your back flyers, sheriff, I think you'll find rewards offered on Sam Steele from Montana and Wyoming. I'd like to put in for them, if you don't mind."

A rueful grin spread on Bell's face. "Then you didn't exactly do this as a free-will offering to the city of Cripple Creek?"

"Oh, but I did, sheriff. Knowing about the rewards was sort of a bonus, you might say." Charity gave the lawman a mischievous wink.

Through the thick stone walls of the jail, Charity heard the squeaky voice of Petey the urchin, recounting events to a gathering crowd. "Gosh, it was somethin'. C. M. Rose just gunned down Sam Steele. Steele gave me this cartwheel not five minutes ago an' now he's laying dead on the floor in the sheriff's office."

"What are your plans now?" Sheriff Bell inquired of the bounty hunter.

"It's too late to catch my train and go after Horsley. That'll have to wait until tomorrow. I'll give that a try, though. Maybe I'll get him and maybe not. After that . . . well, it's been a long time since I've seen Arizona. I might head back to Dos Cabezas."

"What about your interest in the Old Homestead?"

The sheriff's question startled Charity. "When did you find out about that, sheriff?"

"About a month ago." He pulled a long face and gave her a conspiratorial wink. "But that can remain a secret between you and me. What do you say, ah, Miss Charity?"

"Done. Truth to tell, I won't be sorry to shake the dust of Cripple Creek off my boots. I've a feeling, call it a hunch, your union troubles are far from over. I'll stick around until the rewards come in. Then . . . we'll have to see. Good day, sheriff."

Historical Note

Albert O. Horsley, aka Harry Orchard, evaded capture until 1906. Following his successful assassination of Governor Steunenberg of Idaho, he was captured and confined for trial. During his time in jail, Horsley confessed to an amazing string of crimes, including the Vindicator Mine blast and the Independence Massacre.

Horsley received life in prison for his murder of the governor. He was never extradited to Colorado to pay for his crimes. Ironically, it was because the residents blamed the union for paying him more than they blamed Harry for mass murder.

RIDE THE TRAIL TO RED-HOT ADULT WESTERN EXCITEMENT WITH ZEBRA'S HARD-RIDING, HARD-LOVING HERO...

SHELTER
by Paul Ledd

#18: TABOO TERRITORY	(1379, $2.25)
#19: THE HARD MEN	(1428, $2.25)
#22: FAST-DRAW FILLY	(1612, $2.25)
#23: WANTED WOMAN	(1680, $2.25)
#24: TONGUE-TIED TEXAN	(1794, $2.25)
#25: THE SLAVE QUEEN	(1869, $2.25)
#26: TREASURE CHEST	(1955, $2.25)
#27: HEAVENLY HANDS	(2023, $2.25)
#28: LAY OF THE LAND	(2148, $2.50)
#29: BANG-UP SHOWDOWN	(2240, $2.50)

Available wherever paperbacks are sold, or order direct from the Publisher. Send cover price plus 50¢ per copy for mailing and handling to Zebra Books, Dept. 2490, 475 Park Avenue South, New York, N.Y. 10016. Residents of New York, New Jersey and Pennsylvania must include sales tax. DO NOT SEND CASH.

REACH FOR ZEBRA BOOKS
FOR THE HOTTEST IN ADULT WESTERN ACTION!

THE SCOUT
by Buck Gentry

#16: VIRGIN OUTPOST	(1445, $2.50)
#18: REDSKIN THRUST	(1592, $2.50)
#19: BIG TOP SQUAW	(1699, $2.50)
#20: BIG BAJA BOUNTY	(1813, $2.50)
#21: WILDCAT WIDOW	(1851, $2.50)
#22: RAILHEAD ROUND-UP	(1898, $2.50)
#24: SIOUX SWORDSMAN	(2103, $2.50)
#25: ROCKY MOUNTAIN BALL	(2149, $2.95)

Available wherever paperbacks are sold, or order direct from the Publisher. Send cover price plus 50¢ per copy for mailing and handling to Zebra Books, Dept. 2490, 475 Park Avenue South, New York, N.Y. 10016. Residents of New York, New Jersey and Pennsylvania must include sales tax. DO NOT SEND CASH.

BOLT IS A LOVER AND A FIGHTER!

BOLT
Zebra's Blockbuster Adult Western Series
by Cort Martin

#13: MONTANA MISTRESS	(1316, $2.25)
#17: LONE STAR STUD	(1632, $2.25)
#18: QUEEN OF HEARTS	(1726, $2.25)
#19: PALOMINO STUD	(1815, $2.25)
#20: SIX-GUNS AND SILK	(1866, $2.25)
#21: DEADLY WITHDRAWAL	(1956, $2.25)
#22: CLIMAX MOUNTAIN	(2024, $2.25)
#23: HOOK OR CROOK	(2123, $2.50)
#24: RAWHIDE JEZEBEL	(2196, $2.50)

Available wherever paperbacks are sold, or order direct from the Publisher. Send cover price plus 50¢ per copy for mailing and handling to Zebra Books, Dept. 2490, 475 Park Avenue South, New York, N.Y. 10016. Residents of New York, New Jersey and Pennsylvania must include sales tax. DO NOT SEND CASH.

THE TOP NAMES IN HARD-HITTING ACTION: MACK BOLAN, DON PENDLETON, AND PINNACLE BOOKS!

THE EXECUTIONER: #1:
WAR AGAINST THE MAFIA (024-3, $3.50)
by Don Pendleton
The Mafia destroyed his family. Now the underworld will have to face the brutally devastating fury of THE EXECUTIONER!

THE EXECUTIONER #2: DEATH SQUAD (025-1, $3.50)
by Don Pendleton
Mack Bolan recruits a private army of deadly Vietnam vets to help him in his bloody war against the gangland terror merchants!

THE EXECUTIONER #3: BATTLE MASK (026-X, $3.50)
by Don Pendleton
Aided by a surgical face-change and a powerful don's beautiful daughter, Bolan prepares to rip the Mafia apart from the inside!

THE EXECUTIONER #4: MIAMI MASSACRE (027-8, $3.50)
by Don Pendleton
The underworld's top overlords meet in Florida to plan Bolan's destruction. The Executioner has only one chance for survival: to strike hard, fast . . . and first!

THE EXECUTIONER #5:
CONTINENTAL CONTRACT (028-6, $3.50)
by Don Pendleton
The largest private gun squad in history chases the Executioner to France in order to fulfill a bloody Mafia contract. But the killers are no match for the deadly Bolan blitz!

THE EXECUTIONER #6: ASSAULT ON SOHO (029-4, $3.50)
by Don Pendleton
Bolan vows to rid the British Isles of the fiendish scourge of the Black Hand. An explosive new Battle of Britain has begun . . . and the Executioner is taking no prisoners!

Available wherever paperbacks are sold, or order direct from the Publisher. Send cover price plus 50¢ per copy for mailing and handling to Pinnacle Books, Dept. 2490, 475 Park Avenue South, New York, N.Y. 10016. Residents of New York, New Jersey and Pennsylvania must include sales tax. DO NOT SEND CASH.

THE JOKER'S WILDE!

Everyone's just wilde about Larry Wilde, America's number-one bestselling humorist! For hours of guaranteed giggles, order up the wackiest, the wittiest, the very WILDEST of Wilde, from Pinnacle Books!

THE OFFICIAL POLISH/ITALIAN JOKE BOOK	(030-8, $2.95)
THE OFFICIAL JEWISH/IRISH JOKE BOOK	(031-6, $2.95)
THE OFFICIAL BLACK FOLKS/ WHITE FOLKS JOKE BOOK	(032-4, $2.95)
THE OFFICIAL CAT LOVERS/ DOG LOVERS JOKE BOOK	(033-2, $2.95)
THE OFFICIAL SMART KIDS/ DUMB PARENTS JOKE BOOK	(034-0, $2.95)
THE OFFICIAL VIRGINS/ SEX MANIACS JOKE BOOK	(154-1, $2.95)

Available wherever paperbacks are sold, or order direct from the Publisher. Send cover price plus 50¢ per copy for mailing and handling to Pinnacle Books, Dept. 2490, 475 Park Avenue South, New York, N.Y. 10016. Residents of New York, New Jersey and Pennsylvania must include sales tax. DO NOT SEND CASH.